Chasing the Flames

Between Him and Me

Shaheen Kazi

LAUNCHPAD

An imprint of
Srishti Publishers & Distributors

Srishti Publishers & Distributors
A unit of AJR Publishing LLP
212A, Peacock Lane
Shahpur Jat, New Delhi – 110 049

editorial@srishtipublishers.com

First Published by Launchpad,
an imprint of Srishti Publishers & Distributors in 2025

10 9 8 7 6 5 4 3 2 1

This is a work of fiction. The characters, places, organisations and events described in this book are either a work of the author's imagination or have been used fictitiously. Any resemblance to people, living or dead, places, events, communities or organisations is purely coincidental.

Printed and bound in India.

Contents

Acknowledgements

Reflecting on this incredible journey, I am grateful for the unwavering support and encouragement I have received. This journey would not have been possible without the fantastic people who have walked beside me, believed in me, and enriched my work with their contributions and enthusiasm.

To my dear readers, thank you from the depths of my heart. Your love for my work, especially my daring trilogies, has been a beacon of light guiding me forward. Your engagement, feedback, and belief in my storytelling inspire me to keep pushing boundaries and exploring new horizons. Your trust and connection with my stories bring them to life.

I would like to extend a heartfelt thanks to my incredible literary agent, **The BookBakers**. Their dedication, vision, and passion for excellence have been instrumental in transforming my words into meaningful creations. **Mr Suhail Mathur**, the co-founder of The BookBakers, and **Ms Nidhi** have been pillars of support and creativity, ensuring every script shines brightly. Their collaborative spirit and meticulous attention to detail have encouraged me to strive for greatness.

I would also like to express my profound gratitude to my dedicated and dynamic publisher, Srishti Publishers, whose belief in my stories has been truly humbling. **Mr Arup Bose** and his equally efficient team have been an unwavering source of support, bringing my stories to readers with care, precision, and passion.

To my steadfast supporter, mentor, and loving husband,

Rashad, words cannot express how much you mean to me. Your unwavering belief in my vision, guidance, and constant encouragement has been the foundation of my journey. I am truly blessed to have you by my side, championing my work and uplifting me in every moment, from doubt to triumph.

I extend a warm invitation to those who are yet to embark on this literary adventure. As the saying goes, "A writer writes, but the reader completes." Your participation and engagement in these narratives elevate them beyond mere stories, making them a shared experience that I cherish deeply.

Finally, to everyone who has been a part of this incredible journey, thank you for your unwavering support, enthusiasm, and belief in my work. To my wonderful social media followers, your likes, shares, comments, and words of encouragement have been a powerful source of motivation and connection. You are the driving force behind my passion for storytelling, and I am eternally grateful for the opportunity to share my words with such a supportive and inspiring community.

With love and gratitude,

Shaheen Kazi

The wife's ignorance can lead a husband ... to a new love story.

My Wife's Friend

Today, she came home. We moved around each other with an air of studied avoidance, our silence heavy with unspoken thoughts. The attraction hasn't faded; I still feel that pull whenever Maya is near—however, the weight of what we did last month presses down on us both. I only got to know Maya because she is Meenu's closest friend; I was drawn into their orbit after our wedding.

Meenu and I have been married for four years. Our relationship was never a whirlwind romance; instead, it has been a gradual acclimation as we learned each other's rhythms, strengths, and weaknesses over time. I understand that Meenu thrives on connection—she is a social creature who is happiest when surrounded by her friends and family.

Weekends often saw her disappear into a whirl of activities—visits to her parents, shopping trips with friends, and detailed plans that filled her calendar. Her happiness during these moments was essential to me; if this were her way of navigating the world and finding joy, I wouldn't stand in her way. However, these absences created long stretches of quiet in our shared life, silences that I had learned to fill.

As a banker, my work is demanding, providing a ready focus when Meenu is away. I bury myself in the tangible world of projects; the predictable rhythm of process refinement offers a welcome distraction from the echoing silence of those hours. It has become a comfortable numbness—a muted existence where feelings seem dulled. That was until Maya entered my life. She arrived like a sudden burst of colours in a monochrome world, reawakening senses I thought had gone dormant, and directing each flicker of emotion toward her.

I'll never forget Meenu's birthday last year…September 10th, 2024.

Meenu's twenty-sixth birthday celebration. Amidst the familiar faces and party chatter, I saw Maya as if for the first time. It wasn't just that she looked stunning, though she did—draped in a silver silk saree that clung to her form and shimmered with every movement, her bare back catching the light. It was something else, a subtle shift in her usual demeanour, an undercurrent I hadn't sensed before.

She laughed and mingled, graceful, and seemingly at ease, yet my eyes seemed drawn to her against my will. The noise of the party seemed to recede whenever I looked her way, leaving just the magnetic pull she exerted. Her dark eyes seemed warmer and inviting, occasionally meeting mine across the room before I forced myself to look away, unnerved by the intensity of the emotions stirring within me. Each gesture, the way her fingers tucked back a stray curl, sent a jolt through my system, awakening feelings I never knew I had.

Meenu, meanwhile, was the dutiful host, flitting between guests, and managing the celebration. I tried twice to draw her onto the dance floor, but she gently demurred, apologetic, yet firm about her responsibilities.

I found myself watching her move through the crowd, a part of me feeling like an observer rather than a participant in her vibrant world. …

A few brief moments later, she granted me a few short moments, her smile warm as always. But even as I held her close, my mind felt distant, tethered to the image of Maya moving through the crowd. It was a familiar feeling, a slight disconnect when her focus was so outwardly directed.

My glances towards Maya became more frequent, stolen moments of admiration. It wasn't just her beauty; it was an air of quiet confidence, an energy that made her impossible to ignore. She was a force, drawing me in with every graceful movement.

Then Meenu's phone rang, pulling her away from the conversation. I stood alone momentarily, feeling adrift as the party swirled around me. Meenu was always so present for everyone else; sometimes, I wondered where I fit in that constellation of connections, whether I quite measured up. It wasn't a resentment, exactly, more a quiet awareness of the different orbits we seemed to inhabit, even within the same room.

A soft touch on my shoulder made my heart leap. I turned, and Maya was closer than she'd been all evening. The delicate fragrance of her perfume – something floral, intoxicating – enveloped me.

"Mind if I steal you for a moment?" she asked, her voice low.

"Not at all," I managed, hoping my voice sounded steadier than I felt.

The air between us suddenly felt thick and charged. Maya's fingers brushed against mine as she shifted closer, and a sharp, electric jolt shot up my arm. Her gaze held mine, direct yet soft, and for the first time all night, the tension coiled in my gut seemed to ease, replaced by a different kind of fluttering awareness.

This was wrong—deeply wrong. After all, Maya was Meenu's closest friend. But standing there, enveloped in her presence, a traitorous part of me didn't want to pull away. It wanted her closer still. I took a breath, reminding myself to stay composed. My loyalty to Meenu was unwavering, a constant battle against the pull of desire. Nothing could happen. *Nothing else* could happen.

The conversation with Maya was like engaging with a multifaceted gem—her intellect sparkled with sharp insights, her ambition burned with a captivating intensity, and her beauty was the light that illuminated it all. As she shared her business plans, the confidence in her voice was a steady anchor, holding my attention completely. While I offered advice on loans, a familiar process, Maya's quick mind and effortless grace drew me into a fascinating new connection. Her quick mind drew me in with a natural magnetism that transcended mere conversation.

Maya's eyes shone with gratitude when she said, "Thank you for your help. I wasn't sure where to start, but I feel much more confident with your guidance."

Her gratitude brought a smile to my lips, but the spark of ambition in her eyes and the unwavering confidence in her voice truly held my attention. It wasn't just her beauty that captivated me; there was this inner fire, an independence that seemed to echo a quiet restlessness within me, a sense of possibilities I hadn't allowed myself to consider. Part of me genuinely wanted to see her succeed, yet another felt my carefully constructed stability tremble slightly in her presence. The conflict within me was palpable, a battle between my desire to see her thrive and the fear of losing my stability.

We spoke longer, her words washing over me like a gentle current. A growing admiration bloomed within me for her ideas and the elegant way she carried herself. The entire conversation felt surprisingly intimate and deeply personal, as if we shared a history much longer than our actual acquaintance. Her ideas were not just intriguing; they were inspiring, and her elegance was not just attractive but admirable.

Her words were light, but her presence had weight; each

gesture, each smile seemed to hold a quiet depth.

I watched her brush a stray strand of hair from her face, the movement casual yet rendered almost intimate in the room's soft lighting. Her eyes caught mine for a fleeting moment, and something unspoken arced between us, leaving me unsettled, and undeniably drawn to her.

As we spoke, our connection deepened, and I felt as comfortable and charged as if we'd danced all night. I was so caught up in the moment that I barely registered where Meenu was or what she was doing. The time spent in conversation with Maya seemed to evaporate, leaving me wishing for more.

After the last guests departed, Maya stayed behind with Meenu, helping gather stray glasses and plates. I saw Maya in the kitchen later, hair messily tied up, the elegant silver saree now looking beautifully incongruous amidst the post-party cleanup. She looked stunningly real, touchable. A sudden tension coiled within me, a fierce longing to bridge the space between us, to feel the silk of her saree beneath my hands. The impulse was so strong it momentarily stole my breath, but the ingrained boundaries held me rooted. My heart and mind were at war, the desire to be close to her battling with the knowledge of the boundaries I must respect.

While discussing the cleanup logistics with Meenu, the clinking of glasses faded as my attention was snagged by the way the kitchen light caught the silver threads in Maya's saree, a subtle shimmer that held my gaze captive for a beat too long. Caught staring, a wave of heat flooded my face. Flustered, I quickly looked away, and quietly retreated to the balcony. A flush crept up my neck, a betraying heat that spoke of a stirring I hadn't invited, a sense of being adrift on a current I didn't understand. That night, Maya's presence had shifted something fundamental within me, awakening sensations I found both thrilling and deeply unsettling. I was caught in a sea of emotions, unable to fully comprehend the depth of my feelings.

It was past midnight when Meenu suggested Maya stay over.

"She has that ridiculously early flight to Delhi for the fashion show," Meenu explained.

"As her designer, her presence there is essential." Then she turned to me, perhaps noticing my hesitation, "You don't mind, do you? I'd feel better if you could drop her off. It's so late for her to get a cab alone."

"Of course, I'll drop her," I said, my voice hopefully steady. "Don't worry about it. You get some rest."

"Thanks, Dev," Meenu replied, her concern for her friend evident.

"I know you've got work, but I appreciate it. Plus," she added casually, "you and Maya seem to get along well, don't you?"

"Yeah, we're fine," I replied, but the 'fine' was an ocean compared to the single drop of truth I offered. "It's no trouble. You rest up."

A subtle tremor ran beneath my skin, a heightened awareness at the prospect of our solitude, a thrill that felt both exhilarating and forbidden at the thought of being alone with Maya in the quiet cocoon of the car. I asked Meenu if she wanted to come for the pre-dawn drive, but she waved away the idea, citing exhaustion, and urging me to go without her. The opportunity, unsolicited, and sanctioned by my wife, stretched before me like an uncharted territory, filled with anticipation, and a hint of apprehension.

While driving, the city lights blurred into streaks of gold and white, the darkness outside creating a sense of intimacy within the car. Maya had lowered the window, and the cool night air, carrying the faint scent of night-blooming jasmine, stirred her soft curls.

In the dim glow of the dashboard, the silver 'M' on her delicate chain seemed to catch the light like a tiny star against her skin. The quiet hum of the engine was the only sound accompanying the gentle whoosh of the night air. A quiet fascination settled over me as my gaze drifted to her silhouette against the darkness. In the soft light, our eyes met, and her smile held a different quality – a hint of shared intimacy in the stillness of the night, a silent acknowledgement that lingered, feeling more profound than words.

When we reached her destination, she turned, her hand surprisingly soft as it briefly closed around mine. Her brief touch was remarkably potent, a fleeting warmth that lingered on my skin like a phantom limb, a subtle disruption in the familiar rhythm of my senses, and I struggled to maintain my composure.

"Thank you," she murmured, her smile reaching her eyes.

The memory of the soft pressure of her hand in mine, the warmth of her smile, clung to me like the lingering scent of her perfume, a subtle echo in the quiet of my car, even after she released my hand and stepped out.

I replied with a warm smile, "Have a great trip and stay safe."

Back in my car, the familiar melodies on the radio took on a new resonance. Each lyric of longing, each soaring note, seemed to echo the unexpected stirring within me, a secret language my heart suddenly understood. My thoughts drifted back to the image of her—the way the streetlights caught the silver of her necklace, the soft curve of her smile. It was a gentle pull, a persistent undercurrent beneath the surface of my day.

The words on the page blurred as my thoughts circled back to the image of Maya in the soft glow of the dashboard. Maya's memory subtly muted the familiar comfort of my study as if a vibrant hue now coloured what was once monochrome.

What had taken root so quickly about Maya? Had Meenu noticed the shift in my demeanour? The thought of asking Meenu about her friend felt awkward, a breach of an unspoken boundary. Yet curiosity was a persistent hum beneath my thoughts.

During dinner with Meenu, I steered the conversation carefully, mentioning mutual acquaintances before casually slipping Maya's name into the flow. I watched Meenu's reaction, a subtle tension tightening in my chest, hoping my interest wouldn't be too transparent. I framed my inquiry around Maya's bank loan, a flimsy guise for my real question: when would she return? Meenu seemed pleased by my offer of assistance. She immediately contacted Maya, arranging for her to visit me at the bank. After the call, Maya requested my support in obtaining a bank loan. I casually nodded in agreement, but deep down, my heart raced.

The next afternoon, Maya arrived at the bank wearing a beautiful, vibrant floral dress that accentuated her natural grace and charm. Maya's entrance flipped a switch in my office. The muted colours of the room brightened, and a lightness filled the air that had been heavy with routine just moments before. With a neat folder in her hands, Maya exuded an inherently appealing quiet confidence, prepared for anything. As I reviewed her meticulously organized documents, noting her sharp attention to detail, I felt a flicker of admiration beyond the initial attraction. I provided the necessary forms, expediting the process, and wanted to prolong her presence in my office a little longer.

As the last form was signed, a strange reluctance settled over me. I wanted to prolong the easy cadence of our conversation, to hold onto the unexpected lightness she had brought into my day.

"Would you perhaps have time for a coffee?" I asked, trying to keep my tone casual, yet a thread of anticipation wove through my words.

Her warm smile and the easy acceptance in her eyes left a quiet lightness in my chest, a subtle buoyancy that lingered even after she looked away. Leaving the sterile environment of the bank, we found a nearby café, its soft lighting and gentle murmur of conversation creating a more intimate atmosphere. In the soft murmur of the café, the next three hours blurred, each shared glance and murmured word weaving a thread that seemed to exist outside the clock's dominion. I found myself drawn to her radiant presence and how she listened—truly listened, with her attention unwavering, a quality I rarely encountered.

Our connection deepened with an almost imperceptible grace in the following days and weeks. What began as professional courtesy quietly blossomed into something more meaningful, our conversations drifting beyond the sterile confines of the bank. There was a comfortable ease in her company, a feeling of unspoken understanding that grew stronger each day. I cherished these moments and shared pockets of time that felt increasingly significant.

Even in our professional interactions at the bank or during brief phone calls, I made a conscious effort to give Maya my complete attention. I valued providing excellent service to all customers; yet, with Maya, there was an added layer of awareness—a subtle appreciation for her impeccable style. I still remember the unexpected gift of the blue shirt and tie, a thoughtful gesture that spoke volumes about her attention to detail. I was genuinely touched.

A subtle unease began to settle in my chest, a growing awareness that the easy laughter and shared confidences were no longer purely platonic, a path diverging from the familiar into uncharted territory. The easy camaraderie with Maya was subtly shifting, tinged with an undeniable undercurrent of something more profound, something

I struggled to ignore. The complication of her being Meenu's close friend loomed, a boundary I knew I shouldn't cross, yet the pull was becoming increasingly difficult to resist.

One night, while browsing online, a maroon saree with delicate black polka dots caught my eye. The deep red seemed to echo the warmth in her smile, and the small black dots were a playful contrast I could almost see dancing in her eyes. An intuitive sense washed over me, a feeling that this particular saree was meant for Maya and would complement her in a way I couldn't quite put into words. Our connection deepened, evolving into a constant in our lives, a daily exchange that felt essential. I even noticed my style evolving, subtly influenced by Maya's taste—my soft pastel shirts gradually replaced by deeper hues, my routine shifting to include gym sessions and a mindful diet. It wasn't something she ever asked for, yet her presence seemed to shape the man I was becoming. Finally, I felt a genuine surge of happiness as I witnessed Maya's dream materialize with the opening of her boutique, "Maya's Fashion."

Seeing her joy sparked a similar feeling within me, a sense of shedding the predictable skin of the "boring bank manager". When Meenu wasn't around, my phone calls with Maya stretched into hours, time seeming to lose all meaning in her presence. Sometimes, in the brief silences between her words, I caught a fleeting shadow in her eyes, a momentary hesitation in her laughter that hinted at a deeper current beneath her usual composure. Yet, I respected her privacy, hesitant to intrude. However, there was one occasion when... we crossed a line.

It was a quiet weekend night. Meenu's absence had left the house enveloped in an unusual stillness, the silence amplifying the soft echo of my thoughts—thoughts that invariably drifted toward Maya.

Maya had become the quiet anchor in my day, the knowing glance across a crowded room, the anticipated ease of our conversations—a silent language that filled the unspoken spaces, the unspoken smile I expected like the gentle close of the evening. Just as I was losing myself in this familiar reverie, my phone buzzed insistently, breaking the silence.

Her name lit up the screen: *Maya calling…*

I swiped to answer almost before I fully registered what I was doing.

"Would you keep me company for a small event tonight?" Her voice was soft, a delicate uncertainty woven into her invitation.

"Always," I replied, perhaps a bit too quickly, but the sentiment felt utterly true.

With Maya, there was a pull that bypassed any hesitation.

Minutes later, I pulled into her apartment complex parking lot, the glow of the streetlights painting the familiar asphalt in shades of amber. I called her. Two minutes later, the elevator doors opened, and she stepped out. The sight of her felt like a half-forgotten dream coming to life.

She was wearing the maroon saree. The silk shimmered in the dim light, a silent testament to a gift I hadn't dared to hope she'd wear. Seeing her in it was like witnessing a secret unfold; the deep V-neck of the blouse hinted at the graceful lines beneath, stealing the air from my lungs. Each step she took was accompanied by the soft rustle of fabric, a silent poem meant for my gaze alone.

Without a word, she was in my arms. Her embrace was warm and lingering, a gentle pressure that conveyed gratitude, connection, and something neither of us could quite put into words. Her perfume, a delicate floral note, enveloped me like a subtle spell I didn't want to break. We parted slowly and reluctantly, as if disturbing the fragile equilibrium between us.

"I didn't expect you to look so… captivating tonight," I managed, my voice a bit rougher than I intended. A soft smile touched her lips, her eyes holding mine, "I didn't either. But… the air feels different tonight, doesn't it?"

Our interactions at the event felt like a silent ballet of glances and subtle smiles. A shared joke that needed no explanation, a flicker of eye contact during a heartfelt toast—these were the threads quietly weaving an invisible, unbreakable emotional bond.

The drive to her apartment was filled with a silence that hummed with unspoken words, heavy with the weight of our shared moments. When I parked, neither of us moved, the engine ticking softly in the stillness.

"Okay," she whispered finally, turning to me. Her smile was sweet, but a delicate shadow lingered in her eyes.

Before stepping out, she leaned in, her hug softer, and slower this time, reflecting a silent reluctance in the embrace. Then she was gone, walking toward the elevator. Just as the doors began to close, she turned back, her gaze holding mine for a long, suspended moment. I offered a small wave. Driving away, a strange hollowness settled in my chest, a feeling of leaving something vital behind.

The dark streets seemed to whisper her name. Maya… Maya… Maya.

The decision was more an instinct than a thought. My hands turned the wheel, logic fading in the rearview mirror, replaced by the insistent pull of my heart.

I rang her doorbell. The response was immediate, as if she had been listening for that sound. The maroon silk still clung to her like a whispered secret. Her expression was serene, but her eyes held a shimmering anticipation.

"You came back," she breathed, the words barely audible.

"I never really left," I replied, surprised by the truth of my own words.

She stepped aside with a silent invitation. I crossed the threshold, the soft click of the closing door feeling like a quiet punctuation mark at the end of a sentence we were only beginning to understand.

Her big, smoky eyes held mine—a depth of affection that resonated beyond mere attraction. Yet, beneath the love, I sensed a tremor of unspoken need, a vulnerability that quickened my pulse. Her shiny lips, slightly parted, seemed to invite touch, and a silent language unfolded in the quiet space between us.

I reached out, my fingers grazing her cheek, the warmth of her skin a quiet comfort that seemed to settle deep within me. Her eyelids fluttered close as she inhaled, a soft sigh escaping her lips. When her eyes reopened, a flicker of hesitation danced within their depths—a fleeting moment of uncertainty before a more profound desire took hold.

The silence was palpable, a bridge where unspoken emotions flowed freely. I felt the pull, the undeniable yearning that mirrored my own, yet I saw a shadow of conflict in her gaze.

What held her back?

As if sensing my unspoken question, she leaned in, her lips brushing against mine. The first touch was tentative, a soft exploration that slowly deepened, blossoming into something more urgent, more consuming. I held her close, my lips tracing the delicate curve of her neck and shoulder, feeling the subtle tremor that ran through her.

Slowly, carefully, I eased the saree drape from her shoulder, the soft silk whispering against her skin as it unfurled. My fingers grazed her bare arm, and she stood there, the deep V-neck of her sleeveless blouse the only barrier to my touch.

She was undeniably beautiful—a vision that stirred my primal desire. But it was more than just the allure of her body that drew me in; it was the connection in her eyes, the unspoken understanding that lay beneath. She felt like something essential, something I hadn't realized I was missing.

I drew her closer, my arms encircling her smooth waist, my fingers lightly tracing the delicate curve of her spine beneath the thin fabric. Time seemed to suspend, yet a fragile awareness lingered—this moment was fleeting.

When I gently untied the delicate bow of her blouse, it slipped from her shoulders with a soft sigh, revealing the intricate lace of her bra. I lowered my lips to her breast, a tender kiss that elicited a soft gasp, her body arching almost imperceptibly toward me.

Her eyes met mine, and in their depths, beyond the immediate desire, I saw a raw vulnerability—a fleeting glimpse of the emotional weight of this moment.

Her voice, barely a whisper, held a tremor of uncertainty, "Are you sure about this? About us?"

Her words lingered in the air, heavy with unspoken implications, a final moment of hesitation. But her actions became the only answer before I could voice my own tangled emotions. Her lips met mine again—an intense, almost desperate kiss that sealed the unspoken commitment. In that moment, I knew we were on a path we could no longer ignore, that there was no turning back.

The intimacy that followed was unlike anything I had ever experienced—a merging that transcended the physical. We moved together, driven by a force that felt urgent and deeply connected, our bodies speaking a language that words could not express. It was a moment of such profound emotion that it seemed to suspend time.

As the fragile magic of the night faded with the encroaching dawn, a sense of inevitability settled between us. The sun's first rays, painting the edges of the curtains in gold, reminded me that our stolen moment was drawing to a close—a beautiful but unsustainable dream dissolving in the light. I watched the soft rise and fall of her chest beside me, the gentle curve of her lips still slightly parted in sleep. A strand of dark hair lay across her cheek, a delicate shadow in the golden light, and I resisted the urge to brush it away, wanting to hold onto this peaceful image just a moment longer. The warmth of her skin lingered beneath my fingertips, where I had held her close—a phantom sensation that spoke volumes of the night we had shared. A wave of tenderness washed over me, a quiet ache, knowing this fragile beauty was about to disappear with the whole light of day.

When the time came for me to leave, Maya met me at the door. Her embrace was tight, a silent clinging that betrayed a tremor in her arms. A profound quiet had fallen over her, and the unspoken question hung heavy between us. In that moment, the desperate yearning to stay, to erase all other obligations, surged through me. I battled within myself, torn between my love for her and the reality of our situation. I needed only her voice to ask; I would have willingly surrendered my entire world to remain by her side.

Her smoky eyes found mine, and a single tear traced a shimmering path down her cheek. One word, barely a whisper, escaped her lips: "Leave."

The words struck me like a physical blow, yet I knew they were true. What had passed between us transcended passion; it was a profound connection, a fragile bloom that couldn't survive in the light of day.

The unspoken reality of Meenu hung between us—a silent

barrier. I brushed a soft kiss against Maya's forehead, a tender farewell that held the weight of my conflicted emotions.

"I love you, Maya," I whispered—a truth I could no longer hide, and perhaps, a silent goodbye.

Her arms tightened around me, and Maya whispered, "I love you, too," a fragile echo in the morning light.

Walking away that morning felt like leaving a part of my soul behind, a raw ache in my chest.

I should have fought harder, but the path ahead was starkly defined.

Maya became a constant presence in my thoughts—the memory of her eyes, the ghost of her touch, and the echo of our profound connection. But as days bled into weeks, a quiet resignation settled in. We both understood the reality of our situation and accepted it. That night and its bittersweet aftermath would be all we ever had—a cherished memory of a love that could never fully bloom.

She didn't return to my apartment. Her world became the vibrant chaos of fashion shows and deadlines, her life moving on a different trajectory. Yet, her imprint remained, a persistent ache for what could have been.

Each step away from her door that morning was a silent regret. I could feel her presence there, a phantom weight in the doorway. The ending was a shared heartbreak, a quiet acknowledgement of a love that couldn't be.

Time moved on, but the dull ache of her absence remained. The memory of that one night, the sudden, intense experience of true love and its subsequent loss, haunted my quiet moments. Maya remained immersed in her world, her path diverging irrevocably from mine.

It had been three months since that night.

Returning home from work, I found Maya waiting in my living room.

For a moment, everything fell away—the ticking clock, the weight of the day, even my breath. She stood there, poised yet uncertain, and in that instant, it was as if no time had passed. Her dark eyes—those I had once memorized—held something unspoken that pulled at the quiet ache I had buried deep. It was hard to tell whether her visit was for Meenu or me. But one truth hung heavy between us: we couldn't hurt Meenu again. One act of betrayal had already cast a long shadow—a path neither of us could afford to tread once more.

That stolen night with Maya irrevocably altered my understanding of love—an experience etched into the deepest corners of my heart. For that awakening, I would always hold a strange sort of gratitude. She had shown me a depth of feeling I never knew existed.

But the unspoken yet undeniable truth lingered: her heart, in its way, belonged to her friend. That realization deepened my respect for her. Our paths, however intensely they had converged for a brief moment, could not merge.

Perhaps, I now understand, the most valid form of love sometimes demands the hardest choice—the choice to let go. The ache of separation would remain, a constant echo of love held and then released. Because love, real love, isn't always about possession; sometimes, it asks for the quiet strength of sacrifice.

Don't you agree?

My Ex

Once someone becomes an 'ex,' they rarely return. Breakups leave behind echoes—sometimes faint, sometimes deafening—and not everyone moves on easily. Long after it ends, their memory lingers—quiet, persistent, haunting the corners of your heart where silence once lived. Grief didn't crash; it settled, slow, and suffocating.

Before my marriage, there was Alice—my college companion and perhaps the one I never truly understood in time. We shared something real, but in our immaturity, we never treated it as such. When her parents arranged her marriage to a wealthy man, I realized what I had lost. But it was too late by then—a door I hadn't opened was now sealed shut. I was devastated.

Alice came to me before her marriage, hoping to give our relationship one last chance. She pleaded with me to take life seriously and commit to marriage. Although she was willing to leave her engagement and wait for me, I wasn't ready to commit to anyone, as I had never been serious about anything in the past. Sadly, I turned down Alice, and we eventually broke up. The regret of not seizing that chance still weighs heavily on me.

"I'll wait for you, David. Just say the word."

She stood before me, her engagement ring glinting under the dull lights of the hostel, her eyes searching mine for an anchor.

But I had nothing to offer. Not then.

"I can't," I said.

And just like that, I lost her.

Ten years slipped away. Alice vanished from my life as though she had never existed, yet her absence lingered with startling clarity. I can no longer picture her face, but sometimes I wonder—would she recognize mine? The longing hasn't faded. It lives quietly beneath everything, a silent ache I carry, knowing I lost her not to time but to the spaces where I should have loved better.

I've been married to Janice, an architect like myself, for nearly a decade. Our work schedules keep us busy, and we often discuss projects or struggle to meet deadlines. Unfortunately, we haven't had much time to talk about our relationship lately. Janice has always been driven and ambitious, and I admire that. Her career has soared, often outpacing mine, though she never made me feel lesser. However, on certain days, when I return from work, I often feel isolated. When I come home, there's nobody to greet me at the door; my wife doesn't wait for me at the dinner table, and she doesn't seem to care about when I will arrive. Sometimes, I wonder if things would feel different had one of us chosen the quiet over the chase. However, she has refused my request to quit her job and become a homemaker.

After being away from the city for a week, I decided to unwind at a bar following my busy days. Although I was finishing work and leaving the next day, I felt disinterested in returning home, despite having accomplished my tasks. As the days passed, I found myself lost in thoughts of Alice every single night. She consumed my thoughts, and my emotions for her intensified with each passing moment. Despite the conflicting feelings that arose when I thought of her, I found solace in our shared memories. It was as if those memories brought her back to me, and I could feel her presence by my side again. My love for her continued to burn bright; if anything, it only grew stronger each day. The emotional turmoil I was in was overwhelming, but I found comfort in our memories.

I've read somewhere that when a person thinks about someone, *that* person may also become a visitor in their dreams. So, I hoped that Alice dreamed about me too. I tried calling Janice that evening—more out of distraction than genuine desire. She was at her parents' place and didn't plan to return soon. Her voice sounded distant, polite, and utterly indifferent. But my thoughts were not with her; they were with Alice, the woman I longed for, the woman I hoped was thinking of me as I was thinking of her.

Alone with nothing but memories, I finished my drink, and walked toward the elevator. That's when I saw her—a woman stepping ahead of me, her presence oddly familiar. I joined her quietly and offered to press her floor. Then she turned.

It was Alice.

As I stood in the elevator, my mind was a whirlwind—thoughts circling endlessly, some mine, others perhaps borrowed from a past I hadn't fully let go of. At first, I thought it was the resurfacing of Alice—my first love—that was stirring this quiet storm. But when I glanced at her, I saw a familiar look of confusion in her eyes, as if she, too, was lost in some silent storm. She looked as beautiful as ever, her hair falling in soft waves around her face, but her posture was tense, her hands fidgeting with the strap of her bag. We didn't speak. She pressed the button for the fifth floor, and the elevator ascended in a quiet, strained silence.

Seeing Alice again after all these years should have brought joy, or at least nostalgia, but instead, a quiet awkwardness settled between us like dust on forgotten memories. I could have reached for her and told her how much I'd missed her, but she looked at me like I was no one. Her indifference stung me more than I expected. I found myself searching for traces of the girl who once lit up at the sight of me, whose eyes used to see mine in every crowd.

When the elevator reached the fifth floor, Alice exited quickly.

I followed behind, surprised to find her room across from mine. I stood there momentarily, hoping she'd turn around and perhaps say something, but instead, she entered her room, and shut the door.

My heart sank.

There was no reason to stay, so I went to my room and packed my suitcase. As I sorted through my things, I came across an invitation to a buffet dinner hosted by the hotel to celebrate its twenty-fifth anniversary. I considered ignoring it at first—work was my focus, and I had no real reason to go. But then I wondered... what if Alice was attending? Perhaps fate offered me another chance to speak to her, to reconnect, however fleeting.

After hesitating, I changed into something more presentable, quietly hoping to catch a glimpse of her among the guests. But as I stepped out of my room, her door remained closed, silent, distant, and unchanged. I thought about knocking and asking her to join me momentarily, but my nerves held me back. Instead, I walked to the garden alone.

Soft lights illuminated the cosy space where the party unfolded, music played gently, and the rich scent of barbecue filled the air. Usually, I would have taken pictures and admired the setup, but Alice consumed my thoughts tonight. My heart raced as I scanned the crowd, searching for any sign of her, and then I saw her sitting alone under the soft glow of garden lights, her glass of whiskey resting in one hand, her phone in the other. She appeared distant, her eyes focused on the screen, not engaging with the world around her. My heart skipped a beat; maybe this was my chance.

I made my way through the crowd, my footsteps uncertain yet determined. As I neared her, I offered a quiet "Hi," trying to sound as casual as possible, but she seemed startled. Her phone slipped from her grasp, hitting the ground with a soft thud.

Without thinking, I bent down, and picked it up, handing it back to her. As I did, I noticed a familiar sight—photos of us from long ago still lingering in her gallery. She quickly snatched the phone back, a flush creeping up her neck. I stood there momentarily, unsure of what to say, as her sudden discomfort thickened the air.

Alice looked stunning in her red gown. Time had only enhanced her beauty gracefully. Although she had put on a little weight, even that suited her, lending her a softness that made her glow.

I asked if she had company, and she replied casually, "Just me tonight. I'm here for a business meeting."

It was a surprise. Alice in the world of business? It seemed she had taken a path I never expected her to. I stared at her, scratching my head, caught between old memories, and the unfamiliar present.

"Do you still scratch your head when you're confused?" she asked, a trace of amusement lighting up her eyes. Then, she nudged a glass toward me with that same disarming smile I remembered.

"Have a drink with me."

It had been years, yet something about her felt unchanged—genuine and kind. Even after entering the business world, she hadn't lost her softness. That essence of hers—the one I once fell for—still lingered.

As the minutes passed, she began to relax. The stiffness in her shoulders eased with each sip of her whisky. The conversation started to flow, and we revisited some funny and other bittersweet memories. In that gentle exchange, I realized that meeting an ex can open old wounds or offer quiet closure. I was grateful we had chosen the path of maturity. Our words held no blame, only echoes of what once was. For the first time in years, it felt… right.

I wanted to talk to Alice. Strangely, it felt like time had paused—like we had both stepped away from our lives for a quiet 48-hour ceasefire. I thought of asking her about her married life, but the truth was, I wasn't ready to hear the praises of another man.

I'm a practical man. I value moments, not memories, and certainly not pain. Tonight, being with Alice was all that mattered—not the years we lost, not the paths we took, and certainly not her husband.

A soft instrumental melody drifted through the garden, soothing, and rich with nostalgia. I didn't plan it, but I reached out and took her hand, and without a word, she followed me to the dance floor—just like in old times. No questions, no explanations. The music guided us, and for those few minutes, we forgot everything else.

Halfway through the song, her heel snapped. She lost her balance, and instinctively, I caught her—my arms wrapping around her before she could fall. The movement was sudden, and the moment unspoken. But she was close for the first time in a decade—safe, warm, and familiar.

To my surprise, she didn't pull away. She settled against me as if no time had passed at all. We stayed like that longer than we should have. When the music ended, she stepped back, flustered, and offered a sheepish smile.

"Blame the drink," she murmured with a laugh, her voice trying to sound light. I nodded, pretending to agree.

But I knew it wasn't the drink. And so did she.

We returned to the elevator in silence. I secretly wished it would get stuck mid-floor so we could have more time. But it didn't. It arrived too soon.

We exchanged a soft smile as we stepped out. As Alice walked ahead in those broken heels, I couldn't help but gaze at her. Not with lust, but with a silent regret—for not cherishing her more when I had the chance.

As I reached my door, I noticed she was struggling with hers.

The card wouldn't scan, and she sighed in frustration.

I gently offered, "Wait in my room while I sort this out."

She nodded without a word, stepping inside.

When I returned, she was on the balcony, letting the cool breeze wash over her. She looked radiant—almost ethereal—against the night sky. For a moment, I watched her, mesmerized. I wanted to wrap my arms around her, to hold her like I used to, but I reminded myself that this wasn't the past. Still, I walked quietly, and draped a shawl over her shoulders. As I stepped back, she reached behind her, and took my hand firmly.

"Don't go." That's what it felt like she was saying. I didn't.

Instead, I stood behind her, our bodies close, our hearts even closer. She leaned against my chest, and I lowered my head to rest gently above hers. There were no words—just warmth and the ache of a hundred memories between us. At that moment, I felt a mix of longing and restraint, a desire to hold onto her, and a quiet acknowledgement that we couldn't return.

After a while, she turned. Her eyes shimmered—not with desire, but with something more profound. A decade of love, loss, and silence unfolded before us, marked by the indelible imprints of love, the sharp pangs of loss, and the heavy weight of silence.

I cupped her face and kissed her gently—her eyes, cheeks, lips. It wasn't passion. It was comfort. It was closure. It was everything we hadn't said. And in that fragile space between longing and restraint, we held on—if only for a little longer.

Alice wrapped her arms around me, clinging to me as though this embrace could bridge our lost years. I held her tightly, my hands cradling the curve of her back, and for a moment, we weren't just two people from the past—we were two souls that had never stopped waiting for each other.

Inside the room, the silence felt sacred. A soft hum of distant music filtered through the walls, but inside, time seemed to stand still. Our lips met—not in urgency, but with a quiet longing. It was a kiss born from unspoken apologies, missed chances, and memories too tender to forget.

Delicately, I peeled the red dress away from her skin, not as a man claiming something, but as someone unveiling a fragile piece of his history. The fabric whispered to the ground, and when she stood before me, it wasn't just her beauty that struck me—it was her vulnerability. Her eyes searched mine—not for lust, but for answers, for closure, or maybe… for the comfort of still being loved.

We didn't speak as we lay down because our bodies spoke in a language older than time. There was no rush, no firestorm—just warmth, like slipping into a long-forgotten dream.

She traced circles on my skin and whispered, "Do you remember that rainy afternoon when we sat under that broken shelter, and you said nothing but gave me half your sandwich like it was the most romantic thing ever?"

I smiled, my hand brushing softly through her hair. "Of course. You said you were on a diet, then finished both halves."

She giggled—just the way she used to. It was so familiar, so painfully sweet, that it made my throat ache. "And you let me, without even teasing me."

"I was already in love with you, Alice. Teasing would have ruined my chances."

She turned to me, her eyes now serious. "Why didn't we try harder?"

I closed my eyes. The answer was simple, yet cruel. "Because sometimes, love arrives at the wrong chapter. We were the right story… just in the wrong timeline."

Her eyes welled up again; I didn't kiss away her tears this time. I understood that some love stories sting a little, reminding us they were real, so I let the tears fall instead.

"Maybe in another life," she said softly.

"In every life," I replied.

Sometimes, love doesn't need a future—it just needs a moment—a space where it can breathe again, if only for one night. That night, we weren't looking for forever. We were remembering who we were when we were whole.

When the sunlight hit my bed, I realized Alice wasn't there. She had left a note on the pillow stating that she would leave the room in an hour. I checked the time and saw I had only thirty minutes to prepare. I quickly got dressed and got ready to leave the room.

When I arrived at her door, the sight of her packed bags confirmed that she was indeed leaving. With a gentle but firm tone, she rejected my attempt to exchange numbers, indicating she was ready to move on.

Alice explained that staying in touch would be unfair to our partners. She wanted to avoid causing harm to our respective families and ruining her own life. Alice believed that our meeting was not a result of our own will but rather a part of fate's plan. However, she argued that we should not encourage this twist of fate by becoming unfaithful to our partners. I tried to reason with Alice, hoping to convince her not to dwell on these thoughts, but I knew that practicality was not her strong suit. I hugged her tightly and gently urged her to step outside the door. With a bittersweet smile, Alice accepted, and took my hand.

Silently, we made our way to the elevator and waited for the doors to open. However, neither of us wanted to take the elevator. Our time together was running out; Alice would leave in a few minutes, and I would head in a different direction. As the elevator doors opened, we reluctantly stepped inside, the weight of our situation making us feel like strangers.

With a heavy heart, Alice looked at me and whispered, "Let's go."

Alice tried to appear strong, but her tears betrayed the pain of leaving. As I kissed her hand for a final goodbye, the elevator doors slid open with a soft chime. Alice swiped my hand away, her gesture abrupt, but her eyes spoke volumes—more than words ever could.

She picked up her bag and left as if she were a stranger, and I followed, each step heavy with everything unspoken.

Just then, voices broke through the silence, calling our names from opposite directions.

"Alice!"

"David!"

We froze mid-step, the spell between us abruptly broken. For a moment, neither of us moved, caught in the sharp twist of fate that had placed us in this impossible moment.

Janice rushed into my arms and hugged me tightly. "I missed you so much, David," she whispered, her voice full of warmth I no longer deserved.

I turned instinctively to look at Alice, just in time to see her husband press a tender kiss to her soft lips. My heart clenched.

Alice and I locked eyes one last time. But now, something had shifted irreversibly.

To her, I was an ex—a memory folded and packed away.

To me, she would always be the love I never stopped carrying.

The Dancer

"Dream fearlessly.
And
Love unlimitedly"

Every time I entered Jogger's Park, I paused to read those words engraved on the old stone wall near the gate. They constantly stirred something inside me—a longing I couldn't quite name.

Mitali and I have been married for six years now. One truth has stood out in those years: we are worlds apart. Mitali was born into luxury–kitty parties, designer handbags, spontaneous brunches in upscale cafés. On the other hand, I come from a modest middle-class family where second-hand books, simple meals, and evening walks were enough. And somehow, even today, those simple pleasures still are.

Mitali never quite adapted to my world, not the way I tried to blend into hers. I don't blame her for it, though. She has always known comfort, while I have known compromise. Yet, our marriage has lasted—more out of silent endurance than shared passion.

Years ago, I was just an accountant in her father's company. I wasn't someone people noticed—neither suave nor charming, not the kind of man who turned heads. But I was steady. Honest. Maybe that's what caught her father's eye.

Her father, Mr Malhotra, was a man of few words, but the ones he spoke that day changed everything.

When he suggested I marry his daughter, I was stunned. Me? With someone like Mitali?

We couldn't have been more different—our dreams, desires, and even how we drank our morning tea.

I almost laughed, thinking he was joking. But he wasn't. He told me he had been watching me over the years—how I treated others respectfully, never took shortcuts, and showed up every day with quiet determination. That was enough for him.

"You're the kind of man a woman needs," he said, "even if she doesn't know it yet."

His words stayed with me. They gave me a strange kind of hope. Maybe love wasn't always about being perfect. Perhaps it was about being true.

According to Mitali, I wasn't the right man for her—and truthfully, I agreed. She had every reason to feel that way. When we first met, she spoke about her lifestyle, habits, and worldview. I could tell instantly that I didn't fit into any of it. There was no spark, no connection. After that day, the idea of seeing me again—let alone marrying me—seemed unthinkable to her.

But fate had a different plan. Her father's stern ultimatum left her with no choice—either marry me or lose everything—her independence, her wealth, her world. Reluctantly, she agreed. However, she laid down one condition: she wouldn't move into my family home. She wanted her own space.

I didn't blame her. Expecting a woman raised in opulence to adjust to a small, bustling household was unfair. I lived with my parents and younger brother; space was already a luxury.

On our wedding day, amidst flowers, rituals, and well-wishes, I made a silent vow—that if I couldn't earn her love, I would gain her comfort.

But marriage was not a bridge easily crossed.

Mitali cherished designer boutiques and five-star brunches. I found peace in modest meals and grocery bills I could calculate in my head. Mitali curated her world on Instagram; I grounded mine in spreadsheets and morning newspapers. Our differences weren't just visible—we lived them every day.

She drank freshly brewed Colombian coffee; I made my peace with Nescafé. She never checked a price tag; I never skipped one. And yet, none of it made her the wrong person. It meant we walked different roads, trying not to lose the thread that connected us.

That evening, feeling the weight of it all, I walked in the park. Joggers rushed past, children played, and old couples sat hand-in-hand. The breeze carried the scent of earth and eucalyptus. I let it all soak in, circling the park in silence.

As the sun dipped below the horizon, I sat under a tree, lulled by the golden hush of twilight. I didn't notice when someone sat beside me until a gentle "Hello" broke through my thoughts.

She was young, and her voice felt like sunlight filtering through leaves. I smiled and returned the greeting, expecting nothing more. With a gentle smile, she introduced herself as Sonia. Somehow, the conversation flowed. We spoke of trees, birds, and the colours in the sky. She laughed freely, often at her silly yet charming jokes.

I found myself listening closely—not just to her words but also to her energy. It was light and unfiltered.

I remained cautious, not wanting to seem overly eager. Yet, her presence felt like a breeze that quietly, yet undeniably, shifted something inside me.

As I left the park, Sonia handed me a sleek business card.

Her eyes glimmered mischievously, "You look like someone who's lost his smile," she said, tilting her head. "When you feel like tasting happiness–no questions, no guilt–come to this place."

She winked, then turned, and disappeared through the gate.

I glanced down and chuckled.

THE QUEENS CLUB

It's a perfect place for a man in need of cheer.

The tagline was bold and almost playful, yet something about it lingered in my mind longer than I expected. There was no map or website—just a number and a name that felt like a well-guarded secret.

One night, a storm of emotions engulfed me after a heated argument with Mitali. The fight, sparked by her reluctance to visit my parents as planned, left me feeling deeply upset and disoriented. I felt lost in a sea of confusion, desperately needing a sanctuary to regain my balance and find peace. It was a rare moment when I felt disconnected from myself.

"You promised, Mitali," I had said, trying to keep my voice calm. "It's important to me that we go, just this once."

"I'm not your damn puppet," she snapped, her words sharp. "You don't get to control me like that. I have my own life."

The harsh words echoed in my mind as I slammed the door behind me. The house felt colder as I stepped outside, as if the warmth I once felt within those walls had dissipated with the quarrel. It wasn't just the argument that weighed on me; the unspoken frustrations, unmet expectations, and quiet resentments between Mitali and me pressed down heavily on me. All of it came pouring out in one sharp, cruel exchange.

"I never asked for this!" she yelled, her voice cracking. "You never understand me. All you care about is what *you* want. I'm not enough for you, am I?"

Her cutting final words left a bitter taste in my mouth. I could still hear the sting in her voice as she accused me of selfishness, claiming I never truly understood her and couldn't give her what she wanted.

I didn't know where to go or what I wanted anymore. It had been months since I felt this lost, uncertain of who I was and who we were as a couple. As I drove, the journey began as a blur. I didn't follow a specific path or know my destination; I only knew I needed to leave. Every turn felt like a surrender, though I wasn't sure what.

As I passed familiar streets, the houses seemed foreign, and distant. I didn't want to return home yet—too soon, especially with the image of Mitali's frustrated face and disappointed eyes lingering in my mind. The streetlights flickered like tired sentinels, casting long shadows over the road. I needed air, distance—anything to calm the noise in my head.

That's when I saw the glowing sign for The Queens Club. It wasn't just the elegant design or the inviting glow of the lights that pulled me in; it was something more profound. Perhaps it was the promise of solitude or the allure of being somewhere no one knew me, where no one would ask questions I couldn't answer.

A sense of relief washed over me as I approached The Queens Club. I wasn't sure what I sought—peace, escape, or distraction—but it didn't matter. The club, a 35-minute drive from my home, suddenly felt like the perfect distance. As I saw a few men entering, their expressions a mix of seriousness and calm, I felt reassured that I wasn't alone in my need for retreat.

Stepping into the Queen's Club, I immediately felt a stark contrast to my everyday life. The opulence in the air was beyond anything I typically experienced. The leather chairs, reminiscent of those in glossy magazines, and the marble floors, aglow under soft golden lights, create an ambience of unattainable elegance. I couldn't shake the feeling of being an outsider, as if I had stumbled into a world of high-end cocktails and crisp suits I didn't belong in.

I glanced around, my eyes lingering on the price tags attached to everything—the perfectly tailored suits of the men surrounding me, the bottles of wine displayed behind the bar, and the delicate crystal glasses that seemed too fragile to touch. It felt like a place meant for the wealthy, and I could sense the weight of my middle-class roots. The prices were daunting; a drink here could cost more than a week's worth of groceries at home.

But tonight, the cost was irrelevant. I was desperate for a respite, willing to spend time experiencing something different to distract myself from the overwhelming frustration and anger that had been festering inside me.

As I approached the bar, my hands trembled with nerves and anticipation. I didn't bother with the menu or consider the price. I craved something substantial to dull the ache—a way to ease the unresolved tension from the argument with Mitali. I opted for whiskey on the rocks. It was a simple, straightforward choice, but it held the power to soothe my turmoil.

When the bartender placed the drink before me, I didn't consider the cost. For once, I was ready to silence the voice that told me to be careful, to count every penny, and to save for a rainy day. It wasn't a night for caution; it was a night to escape the world for a few hours, to feel like someone else, and to shed the weight of responsibility and frustration.

I took a slow sip, feeling the warmth spread through my chest. It was expensive, but it was exactly what I needed—what I wanted. And for tonight, that was enough.

The sound of businesspeople hustling and mingling added to the tense atmosphere. Men congregated around the main stage every night to witness a spectacular performance. The men were visibly excited, holding bundles of hundred-dollar bills, eagerly anticipating the appearance of the exotic dancers. Even though the music thumped loudly, I could make out some men gambling in a nearby corner and others sitting at the bar, drinking heavily, or chatting with the women.

I felt like an outsider. The world around me was full of affluence and indulgence, everything foreign to my simple, middle-class life. The prices of the drinks alone made me second-guess every decision I made that night. I couldn't help but compare everything I saw to my modest lifestyle—how I could barely afford a dinner at a small local restaurant, let alone a night out here. Yet, tonight, I had already let go of my inhibitions. My emotions, raw from the argument with Mitali, pushed me to experience anything that could make me feel different, even if only for a few hours.

The women were stunning, with their slim frames, curvy hips, and large, round breasts that seemed to bounce around as they performed their topless routines. The performers at the Queen's Club were predominantly white, which caught my attention due to their beauty and because it seemed to be an unspoken expectation. The men here seemed to have only one type of woman they desired—the busty blondes I had only seen in adult films or magazines. In person, it was overwhelming.

A strange feeling crept up inside me as I stood there, part awe, part unease. I had never been in such an extravagant environment, and though I tried to ignore it, I could feel the disparity between me and the others. The sumptuous shows and endless money made me question why I was here. But the anger and frustration I had been carrying made me shut out those thoughts, even if just for tonight.

Then, as the noise around me grew louder, I realized something. The club wasn't just a place for men to watch women dance; it was also a place for women to perform. It was a place where people paid for happiness, or at least a temporary escape from reality. The price tag was steep, but the club seemed to operate on the belief that money could solve everything—even loneliness. If you had enough money, it didn't matter how you looked or who you were. You could buy the company of beautiful women, the attention, the fleeting connection.

But as the night wore on, I couldn't shake the uncomfortable feeling gnawing at me. Being in this place wasn't who I was, and I knew it. As much as I craved something different, this wasn't the answer. I wasn't here to be someone I wasn't, and as I turned to leave, I promised myself I wouldn't return to this world again.

As I was getting ready to leave the club after a long night of partying, my eyes landed on the billboard with Sonia's name. She was the next performer, and I suddenly found myself wanting to stick around and watch her. I wondered if she was as good as people claimed she was and if her music could move me like everyone said it could. However, I was also tired and ready to go home, so I didn't know what to do. Just as I was about to make a decision, a drunken man stumbled up to me and started slurring his words. He asked me to stay and watch Sonia's performance with him, promising it would be worth it. I hesitated momentarily, unsure if I should trust him, but then I realized I didn't have the same financial security as the others who frequented the club. The luxurious atmosphere was alluring, but it was a facade that masked the underlying reality of my situation.

He looked at me, waiting for a response.

I hesitated, then said, "Look, I'm not like the others here. I don't have the kind of money they throw around. If I make one wrong move, I could lose everything I've saved."

That drunk man laughed and understood it was my first visit to that club, so he gave me a golden ticket from his pocket and said, "I like your simplicity as you are a first-time visitor; being the devil of this hell tonight, you are my guest. So, all your drinks, food, and entertainment are on me. So go, young men; enjoy your life tonight. At least before you die, you'll have something nasty to remember."

The gentleman's kindness deeply touched me, and I felt a sense of gratitude as I received the shiny golden ticket from him.

The devil's manners were impeccable. *If all villains are this polite, I'm switching sides.*

With a smile on my face, I turned around and made my way back to catch Sonia's much-awaited performance. As I entered the club, I was greeted by a lively atmosphere, with laughter, and music filling the air. Apart from the lead artist, The Queens Club had a group of twenty other charming ladies responsible for ensuring that all the guests had a wonderful time. The ladies walked around the venue, engaging in friendly conversations with the patrons and providing them with various services, including serving drinks, and offering a more intimate experience by sitting on their laps. At the end of the night, the servers charged the appropriate amount and then bid farewell to the guests.

These girls were the perfect answer to the accumulated sexual frustration that men like me needed to release. So, I placed the golden ticket on my table and ordered a few tequila shots. Upon seeing my golden ticket, a waitress invited me to sit in an exclusive seat just off the stage.

The main stage had a booth set up, and the audience eagerly awaited the performance. Then, the announcer declared that Sonia would soon take the stage.

Before the band's performance could begin, the stage went dark, and an orange projector lit up the area. To my surprise, it wasn't jazz music playing but a Bollywood remix of a beloved song from my teenage years. The familiar melody caught my attention and made me want to get up and move.

The unusual sounds captivated the men's attention, sparking excitement in their minds and hearts. I was among them, curious who would dance to the exotic music played on stage.

The crowd fell completely silent as a hand began to pull back the curtain. Everyone focused on the scene unfolding before us. Suddenly, an exotic beauty appeared, showcasing smooth skin, long, silky hair, and brown eyes. Sonia wore a sari that flowed gracefully over her form, teasing the line between modesty and allure—a delicate veil of fabric that left much to the imagination. I had never seen a sari draped in such a manner before in my life. Sonia's body was only partially covered, offering a tantalizing glimpse of her delicious curves while revealing part of her right breast. The outfit's waist-high slit concealed only a portion of her muscular leg, with a thin sheer layer enhancing the allure. Sparkling diamonds and gold adorned her hands, neck, and ears—a treasure unlike any I had ever seen.

As Sonia danced seductively around the stage, she tried to cover her privates with her sari, her hips moving sensually to the music. Her fluid and hypnotic movements held the room captive as if time had paused to watch. The entire audience was entranced by her, eagerly anticipating her next move. I had never felt such a high level of sexual tension; every man was utterly captivated by Sonia.

When she finished her performance, the crowd erupted in applause. Standing statuesque on stage, the stunning dancer accepted the praise with a self-aware smile. Throughout the night, it was clear that she understood her impact on all of us.

The men in the room began rummaging through their wallets, ready to place bids to see who would have the opportunity to take that exotic beauty home. Knowing I wouldn't get along with those business types, I left. It saddened me to think that an obscene and greedy businessperson would claim such a lovely treasure.

I greatly admired Sonia's beauty and appreciated it more than anyone else in the room. Despite wearing very little clothing, she still managed to look stunning, almost like a beautiful doll. Something different and captivating about her caught my attention.

Just as the bidding session was about to start, the host abruptly appeared, bringing the proceedings to a halt. Instead, he announced that Queen Sonia would spend the entire night with me as a special guest at the club. The announcement startled me, and I noticed the frustrated expressions on the faces of the wealthy men around me. At that moment, I felt like the contest winner; it was as though I was the hero surrounded by vultures waiting for the final moments of their prey. I was the house winner that night, a rare instance for someone like me who had never previously won anything.

As the surprise washed over me, my eyes instinctively found the drunken man who had given me the golden ticket. He shot me a mischievous wink and made a subtle gesture, encouraging me to enjoy the night and confirming his unexpected role in this turn of events. Trying to play it cool in front of everyone, I took a sip of my drink, strolled around the room, and heard voices saying, "Congratulations."

As I walked toward Sonia's front door, my heart raced with a mix of excitement and anxiety. I had been looking forward to this evening for days and could hardly believe that such a stunningly beautiful woman had agreed to spend time with me. When she opened the door, I was momentarily at a loss for words, but we quickly exchanged greetings and reintroduced ourselves. Sonia seemed thrilled to see me at the club and promised to make my night wonderful.

I tried to control my emotions and maintain some distance, but Sonia was determined to break the ice. She asked me about myself and shared interesting anecdotes from her life. Her warm and friendly demeanour put me at ease, and I gradually relaxed.

Despite my initial hesitant nervousness, I couldn't help but smile as she spoke. Her eyes, sparkling with humour, and intelligence, captivated me, and I found myself drawn to her. Although I tried to avoid direct eye contact, I couldn't resist stealing glances at her occasionally.

Queen's singing at the Queen's Club had been enjoyable, but as it came to an end, I found myself in a bit of a predicament. I hadn't planned ahead and now didn't know where to take Sonia. Anxiety surged within me as my mind raced for possible solutions. Sensing my distress, Sonia kindly offered to let me stay at her place for the night. I was grateful for her generosity and accepted her invitation with a smile.

While driving to Sonia's house, I noticed how quiet the street was. I couldn't help but remain silent, unsure of what to say. The silence was awkward, but Sonia seemed understanding and didn't push for conversation. During the drive, I reflected on how kind she had been to me, and I felt grateful for her company.

When I pulled outside Sonia's apartment, a wave of nerves, and anticipation washed over me. I had imagined this evening for weeks, and now that it was here, I only wanted to make a genuine impression.

Inside, Sonia gestured toward the couch. "Make yourself comfortable. I'll get us something to drink," she said softly.

I nodded, settling in, and tapping my fingers against my knee as I watched her move toward the bar.

My thoughts raced—*what would we talk about? Would I be able to relax?*

She returned with two glasses and handed me one of them.

"To unexpected meetings," she said, clinking her glass against mine.

"To honesty," I replied, unsure why those words came out, but they felt right.

There was a moment of quiet as we sipped our drinks. Then Sonia looked at me, her eyes softer than before. "You're tense," she said gently. "Don't be. This isn't... what you might think it is."

I tried to smile, "I was just not used to this kind of intimate evening."

She chuckled. "Neither am I. Not like this. Not when someone listens."

Her gaze lingered for a moment. "I can't bear the thought of anyone else being around me," she confessed, her voice trembling. "Even for a minute, I feel... invaded."

That vulnerability hit me hard.

"I get that," I said. "I feel like I've been living in someone else's world for too long."

She tilted her head. "You're not like the others. I noticed that the first time I met you was at the park. You were... just there. No pretence."

I gave a small laugh. "So you gave your card to a stranger with no pretence?"

"Well," she grinned, "you looked like someone who wouldn't misuse it."

I felt my throat tighten and checked my phone without thinking. There were no messages or calls.

She noticed. "Is someone waiting for you to come back?"

"Not anymore," I replied quietly. "I don't think she even noticed I left."

She reached over and took my hand gently. "You don't have to do anything tonight."

I looked down at our hands. "Thank you... that means more than I can explain."

I hesitated before continuing. "I guess I'm here because I needed to feel like I mattered to someone."

Her expression softened further. "You do."

We talked more about our lives, our regrets, and the silence of things we never dared to say. Sonia told me about the night her father left this world and how, at that moment, a part of her childhood died, too. She didn't get time to cry—only to carry. Some people learn to walk, while necessity compels others to stand in the face of danger. Life didn't wait for her to be ready. It just handed her grief and called it growing up.

"I dropped out of college to work at Queen's Club," she said. "Someone had to earn, someone had to pay the fees."

I nodded. "You did what many wouldn't. You gave up your dreams so someone else could chase theirs."

She smiled faintly. "Maybe. But sometimes I wonder if I lost too much of myself in the process."

"We all lose parts of ourselves," I said. "Some of us are just lucky enough to find someone who helps us pick them back up."

The night went on. We shared drinks, danced to old Bollywood tunes, and laughed at memories that felt oddly familiar.

By the time silence returned, it was no longer uncomfortable. It felt like understanding.

As the night progressed, our chemistry deepened, and we started to connect more profoundly. The attraction was undeniable.

As the night grew quieter, I poured myself a glass of wine and watched Sonia dance by the window. The moonlight shimmered on her jewellery, and her movements were fluid and mesmerizing.

She wasn't just beautiful—she was art in motion.

"You dance like you own the night," I said, my voice barely above a whisper.

She glanced over her shoulder, a smirk on her lips.

"Maybe I do. But tonight, I'm dancing for you."

Her diamond and gold jewellery sparkled like stars, and her movements were graceful, almost as if she were floating. With every sway of her hips, a shiver ran through me, igniting a fire within the room. To calm myself, I slowly undid the top button of my shirt.

She noticed, of course. Her eyes twinkled as she moved closer, her sari trailing behind her like a silken wave.

"I see you're getting hot," Sonia teased, her voice low, and playful.

I chuckled, trying to maintain my composure. "You have that effect on me," I replied, my eyes tracing the curves of her body as Sonia approached. Her presence became more intoxicating with each step.

She knelt before me, her touch sending sparks through my body. Her hands gripped my thighs firmly, and her breath was warm against my skin.

"I want you," she whispered, her lips so close to mine that I could feel the moist heat of her breath ghosting over my skin, a shiver tracing its path down my neck. The scent of her – a heady blend of warm skin and something musky and intensely personal – filled the small space between us, igniting a fire low in my belly.

Her dark and dilated gaze locked onto mine, a raw hunger in its depths mirroring the sudden, fierce ache within me. Her hand, no longer hesitant, slid up my chest, her fingertips grazing the hard line of my pectoral muscle before settling possessively over my heart. Its frantic rhythm betrayed my carefully constructed composure.

My own hands found her waist, my thumbs pressing into the small of her back, drawing her closer until the soft swell of her breasts brushed against my chest, a jolt of pure sensation shooting through me. I could feel the rapid beat of her own heart against my palm, a frantic drumbeat echoing my desire.

Her breath hitched again, a soft gasp that mingled with mine, and the anticipation stretched taut and electric between us. The air crackled with unspoken needs, a silent demand for the merging that felt inevitable and desperately craved. Her lips parted slightly, a quiet invitation, and at that moment, the world narrowed to just the two of us, poised on the precipice of something consuming and utterly authentic.

Our relationship was undeniable, almost magnetic, and as our bodies became one, it felt like the world had disappeared. There was only Sonia and I. I could feel her warmth, passion, and every inch of her as she moved in time with me, taking control when she needed to and letting me lead when she wanted to.

"Slow down," I whispered, though I could feel how much she wanted to push us both to the edge.

But Sonia knew me too well. She smiled, with a knowing glint in her eye, and gave me what I needed, letting the pace ebb, and flow as we lost ourselves in the moment.

The night stretched on, our bodies entwined, passion consuming us, yet beneath the heat, something more profound was growing.

Afterwards, we lay together, our bodies drenched in sweat, still tangled in each other's arms. Our kisses turned soft, slow, and lingering. It was no longer just about the fire between us; it had evolved into something real and lasting.

As time passed, our bond grew stronger. We became inseparable, and our connection blossomed into something far more meaningful than mere physical attraction. We started seeing each other every week, exploring the city's nightlife, sharing quiet moments at the jogging park, and enjoying dinner together while talking about everything and nothing at all.

It didn't take long to realize that I couldn't imagine my life without her. Our emotional connection was something I had never experienced before. She made me feel alive like no one else ever had. Months later, I made a decision that changed everything: I asked Mitali for a divorce. It wasn't easy, but I explained my reasons to her. As painful as it was, she agreed, and I left to start a new chapter in my life—one where Sonia and I could genuinely build something meaningful together.

We started fresh. We got jobs, found our place, and embraced a life free of pretences. It was never about money or status, but the simple joy of being with someone who truly understood me.

Sonia and I had discovered something rare and pure. Fate brought us together—two lonely souls searching for something real. With her, I finally understood what love truly was and gained a new perspective on life.

"Dream fearlessly. Love without limits," I whispered, as we lay beneath the open sky, the rest of the world quietly fading away.

Naughty at 40

A few days ago, I crossed into my forties. Quite the milestone, right? My fortieth birthday is one I'll never forget. Let me provide some background if you're curious about me or my life.

My name is Wilson, and I am a musician. I'm part of a rising talent group that keeps me busy most days, strumming my guitar in the studio or performing at weddings and private gatherings. It's a good life—music pays the bills, and there's something magical about being part of someone's special moment.

At home, I'm a family man with a wonderful wife, a young son in school, and a ridiculously handsome dog who thinks he owns the place. Nancy, my wife, and I have been married for ten years. Once upon a time, our love life was straight out of a romantic ballad. There wasn't a single night when we didn't get lost in each other, sharing tender touches, whispers, and kisses that lingered well past midnight. We found comfort in cuddling and quiet intimacy, even on her off days.

But as they say, good things evolve, and sometimes fade.

Nancy changed after our son was born. Once, we shared everything so freely, but her love began to focus entirely on motherhood. I have always admired her devotion. However, along the way, we lost what we had together. Our once-electric chemistry began to fade. Passionate nights transformed into gentle goodnights, and our sex life quietly disappeared. She used to initiate intimate moments, but now she's always too tired or preoccupied with our son.

To the world, we appear to be the perfect couple—taking vacations twice a year, sharing laughter over coffee, and attending school plays hand-in-hand. But behind those smiles, we both carry an unspoken truth: we've become partners in parenting rather than lovers.

I never resented her for the shift. I held on to hope, believing that those dry nights would pass and that the spark would return on its own one evening. For many of us, that kind of hope never truly fades.

Yet, as time passes, I've noticed a different tune in our silence. I'm uncertain about what the future holds for us, but I know I'm not ready to give up on our love.

However, the wait has grown longer than I ever imagined. Nancy's interest in intimacy seems to have vanished entirely. Her world now centres around our son's meals, schoolwork, and bedtime routines. When night falls, she wants to sleep. It's a harsh reality that many of us face.

One night, I reached for her—gently, longingly. She allowed me to kiss her and touch her, but when I tried to go further, she stopped me. There was no explanation, no anger—just a quiet rejection that left a bruise deep inside me. We didn't talk much after that. I attempted to connect with her again a few days later, hoping she would meet me halfway. But Nancy looked at me and said, "I can't."

It was a simple sentence, yet it carried the weight of a thousand cold nights. Nancy still kissed me, hugged me, and showed her love in familiar, domestic ways, but a wall had formed between us. The closeness we once shared had quietly faded. Even the rare attempts we made to reconnect now ended in discomfort or pain for both of us.

I understood that she was exhausted and that motherhood

had changed her. But I couldn't pretend I wasn't lonely. This loneliness, this longing, was a struggle I faced every day. It became a journey of personal growth, learning to cope with the changes in our relationship and finding ways to express my feelings without causing her more distress.

She knew. Of course, she did. However, we never really discussed it. The subject made her uneasy. How could I explain that I missed not just her touch but the connection—the fire we once shared?

It had been two years since we last made love when I ran into my college ex at a wedding gig. She was as beautiful and confident as I remembered. We laughed and shared stories, and for one night, I gave in. The encounter wasn't something I planned; it wasn't love. It was like a starving man tasting warmth again.

The next day, while sorting laundry, Nancy found an open packet of condoms in my coat. She didn't yell or accuse me.

Instead, she held them up and asked, "Was it someone you know?"

I didn't lie. It's easy to weave falsehoods with those who don't hold your heart, but honesty felt like the only path with Nancy. I told her the truth—that it was a one-time thing, a mistake, a moment I didn't plan on repeating. Nancy cried—quietly and heartbreakingly—for days. I hated myself for what I had done and even more so for the pain it caused her.

But then something unexpected happened. Nancy came to me and said, "I forgive you."

She didn't stop there. "If being with someone else helps you... I won't stop you. Just don't fall in love with her, and don't let her expect more than what it is."

I stared at her in disbelief. That moment broke me more than her tears. I told her I didn't want anyone else, that it wasn't about sex—it was about us. But she just smiled a tired, understanding smile. So, following Nancy's unexpected words, a strange new chapter began in our marriage. I accepted it, not because it was what I wanted, but because it was what we needed.

In the past two years, I've been with six women. It never meant anything, and it never lasted. I always returned home to Nancy. But I carry guilt—because no matter what permission Nancy gave me, this isn't the life I wanted for us. The guilt and the conflict within me serve as constant reminders of the love I still hold for Nancy and the pain I have caused her.

Despite the complexities of our present, I still long for something simpler… something closer… something like before. The memories of our closeness and quiet intimacy linger—bittersweet reminders of all that we once were.

One day, I addressed an ongoing issue by taking my wife to a counsellor. While I was planning this, a colleague called with exciting news about an upcoming Bollywood event.

"David, listen! Don't even think about missing this! It's a big one! We're performing in Goa!"

My friend's voice was filled with excitement, and I could feel his enthusiasm. The event's payout was significant, so I agreed to host it and began making preparations.

However, shortly after, one of our female singers was involved in an accident and would not be able to perform. As a result, we needed to find a replacement singer for the event.

We held auditions for singers every day, but I never felt genuinely delighted by any of them. I was searching for a voice with that special magic—one that could immediately connect with listeners whenever she sang. I spent a considerable amount of time searching for a voice that would appeal to people of all ages, but despite listening to many voices day and night, I couldn't find one that impressed me.

As the deadline approached, tensions within our group escalated over the decision-making process. We had only one day to finalize our choice and complete the other preparations. To move forward, I decided to select someone for the role.

One afternoon, I heard a melodic hum while taking a break and relaxing in my chair. I opened my eyes but didn't see anyone around, and the humming persisted. I could hear every low and high note with beautiful clarity emanating from a sharp, perfect voice.

Her high-pitched voice caught my attention, distracting me from my task. I saw a young girl, likely in her twenties, humming with her headphones. When she noticed me, she stopped humming, and removed her headphones. I encouraged her to relax and invited her into my studio.

As she walked in, her astonishment was evident. The fear and tension that once marked her face had melted away—she looked relaxed, almost at ease. She introduced herself as "Ayesha." I told her I had already recognized her talent and that the audition was merely a formality in front of the group. When she began to sing, her voice captivated everyone. The musicians broke into spontaneous applause. Their unanimous praise, a powerful testament to Ayesha's talent, welcomed her as the newest member of our group.

The days passed smoothly as I kept busy with rehearsals and planning. There were nights without intimacy, so many that I gradually stopped thinking about sex altogether. I became so lost in my thoughts, so tuned into my body's silence, that desire faded into the background. Finally, the day arrived when we all reached Goa and began preparing for the event. I found Ayesha to be quite friendly and impressed by her youthful energy. She was a talented and ambitious girl, especially in singing. I always paid close attention when she sang; at times, she would give me playful winks and smiles while we performed together, which I didn't mind.

On the last day of the event, we had a double celebration. I had two reasons for enjoying that evening so much. First, the event had been a tremendous success, and the other organizers invited our band to perform at future events. Secondly, it was my fortieth birthday, which I celebrated with my band. We enjoyed a night filled with music and drinks. During the celebration, I was amazed to discover that Ayesha possessed exceptional skills in both singing and dancing. She performed a captivating belly dance just for me, and I couldn't help but be mesmerized by her graceful movements.

Drinks played a significant role in my birthday celebration, and Ayesha's dance gave me quite a thrill. I tried not to look at her with lustful thoughts—I didn't want history to repeat itself with another one-night stand.

The party was in full swing, with everyone enjoying the drinks and the lively atmosphere. Amidst the festivities, Ayesha surprised everyone by arriving with a birthday cake. Though she was the only one who had planned for it, the message on the cake read,

"Happy B'day Naughty 40… "

Her thoughtful gesture touched me, and I hugged her to express my gratitude. As I held her close, I could feel her body against mine, and she gently kissed my cheek while whispering, "Happy Birthday, Sexy. Let me be your gift tonight"

The strong scent of roses and her inviting gaze had a profound effect on me. However, I chose to maintain a sense of innocence, pretending to be unsure of her romantic signals and instead opted to tease her a little.

The party was enjoyable, but it was time for everyone to

return to their respective rooms. My friends were exhausted and ready to sleep, so we all said our goodbyes and went to our rooms. Unfortunately, I did not find Ayesha anywhere at that time; perhaps she had left for her room, I thought.

After returning to my room, I heard a knock at my door. I opened it to check and saw Ayesha standing in a loose satin gown with a long, deep neck. The material was so fine that I could see her skin underneath the fabric. She wore nothing underneath her dress; the lace border seemed beautiful, set off by a V-neck. Her long black hair was streaming over her shoulder, and her eyes were full of lust as she looked at me. Her cleavage was overflowing with a deep breath.

The click of the closing door was the only sound as she entered my room. Her gaze held mine, silently acknowledging the unspoken tension that had been present all evening.

"David," she finally murmured, her voice a soft melody that seemed to resonate within the sudden quiet, "I couldn't stop thinking about the way you looked at me tonight."

A slow smile spread across my face, the anticipation tangible.

"And what did you think of the way I looked at you, Ayesha?" I asked, my voice dropping to a low murmur that felt intimate in the stillness.

Ayesha drew a slow breath, her chest's subtle rise and fall a captivating rhythm in the quiet.

Her gaze held mine, a vulnerability flickering within its depths. "It made me feel… seen, David. Truly seen, in a way I haven't felt in a long time."

A smouldering heat shimmered in the air between us, mirroring the quickening pulse in my veins. Ayesha's fingers, delicate and deliberate, found the knot at her shoulder. The silk of her gown whispered as it slid, revealing a tantalizing glimpse of skin beneath. Her gaze never left mine as she slowly traced the lace at the neckline, a silent invitation. With a final, graceful movement, the gown pooled at her feet, leaving her standing before me, her beauty unveiled in the soft light.

A soft gasp escaped me. "You're breathtaking, Ayesha," I whispered, my fingers lingering a little longer than they should on her cheek, the heat of her skin igniting a slow-burning fire inside me.

A playful smile curved her lips, a spark of mischief dancing in her eyes. "You're not so bad yourself, David," she murmured, her eyes tracing mine with quiet fire.

"Looks can be deceiving, you know. I'm not just what you see."

A chuckle rumbled in my chest, my heart thrumming a faster rhythm.

"Indeed," I replied, my gaze holding hers, silently acknowledging the depth I sensed within Ayesha.

My guitar lay on the nearby couch. Ayesha picked it up with fluid grace, cradling it like a cherished possession. Standing before me, the warmth radiating from her naked skin was a stark contrast to the cool, smooth wood of the guitar she held, a visual, and tactile paradox that heightened my awareness of her vulnerability and the unexpected intimacy of the moment. Ayesha lightly strummed a few chords, and the soft music filled the charged silence. As she turned, the curves of her body moved with the gentle rhythm, an unspoken invitation to explore her melody.

"That's... beautiful, Ayesha," I murmured, my voice thick with awe and a stirring I couldn't quite name. Was it the melancholic beauty of the tune, born from those elegant, perfectly manicured fingers, that held me spellbound? Or was it the almost dreamlike vision of her, stripped bare of pretence, utterly lost in her private world beneath the hushed glow of the night? I couldn't decipher the artistry or raw vulnerability that captivated me more.

A playful smile danced on her lips as she gently placed the guitar back on the couch. Her eyes met mine, filled with an unspoken promise, "Thank you, David. But tonight, I have a different kind of music in my mind."

The unspoken language in her eyes intensified as she moved towards me, each step a deliberate invitation.

"I have a feeling," she murmured, her voice a soft caress that held both a playful tease and a deep longing, "this is going to be a night we won't forget."

A warmth bloomed in my chest, a feeling of inevitability mingling with anticipation.

"I have a feeling you're right," I replied, my smile mirroring the unspoken promise in Ayesha's gaze.

Her hands found mine, guiding one to the soft curve of her breast and the other to the flare of her hip.

"Do you feel that, David?" she whispered, her breath ghosting against my ear.

A tremor ran through me, a response I no longer tried to suppress. My fingers tightened slightly, a gentle exploration of the yielding warmth beneath my touch. "That's... a shadow of how I feel every time you're near, Ayesha."

A soft groan escaped her lips as her eyes drifted closed, a surrender to the sensations building between us. I leaned in, my lips tracing a slow path along the delicate curve of her neck, the scent of her skin intoxicating. Lower, I tasted the soft swell of her breast through the delicate lace of what remained of her attire.

Her hands then moved to my shirt, her touch feather-light as she eased it over my head. Then, the rasp of my jeans unfastened filled the quiet. Her fingers brushed against me, a fleeting, electric touch that sent a jolt of pure sensation through me. Her lips followed a warm, fleeting caress that stole my breath.

"You're making it hard to think," I murmured against the warmth of her skin.

"Good," she teased softly, her breath warm against my lips. "I want you to feel what I feel, David. This heat... this need. It's been waiting for so long."

The air crackled with a heightened awareness, and every breath we took seemed to mingle together. Her dark eyes, filled with a raw desire, held mine, and in their depths, I saw a reflection of my yearning. Without breaking our gaze, I reached out, my hands slowly tracing the delicate curve of her shoulders. The smooth warmth of her skin was a stark contrast to the cool night air. My thumbs gently brushed against the sensitive skin at the base of her neck, eliciting a soft shiver that ran through her.

She mirrored my touch, her hands finding their way to the nape of my neck, her fingers tangling lightly in my hair. A sigh escaped her lips, a sound that spoke volumes of the restraint she had been holding onto.

Leaning closer, I brushed my lips against hers, a feather-light touch that was more promise than possession. Her taste was intoxicating, a blend of sweetness, and a hint of something wild.

"Ayesha," I murmured against her mouth, the sound thick with desire, "this... this feels like something I've waited for without even knowing it."

Her grip on my neck tightened slightly, a silent affirmation. "Me too, David," she whispered, her breath warm against my lips. "It's like... coming home to a place I never knew existed."

The space between us dissolved completely. Our lips met again, this time with a more profound urgency, a silent claim that spoke of our intense connection. The kiss was a language of its own, conveying the unspoken desires, and the pent-up emotions that had been simmering beneath the surface.

My hands moved from her shoulders, exploring the delicate curve of her back and the smooth expanse of her skin. Her body moulded against mine, a perfect fit that sent me a fresh wave of heat.

Her fingers tightened their hold on my hair, guiding my mouth back to hers. The kiss deepened, becoming more demanding. It was a dance of unspoken needs, a silent conversation conducted through touch and breath.

Driven by a mutual urgency, the kisses became deeper, tongues tangling in a silent exploration. My hands slid down Ayesha's back, settling on the curve of her waist, pulling her closer until there was no space between us. I could feel the rapid beat of her heart against mine, a frantic rhythm that echoed my own.

Her hands left my hair; instead, she pressed them flat against my chest, the warmth of her palms seeping through my skin. I could feel the subtle tremor in her touch, a testament to the intensity of her emotions.

Breaking the heated kiss, I trailed soft kisses down her jawline to the sensitive curve of her neck, the scent of her skin intoxicating. She arched slightly, a soft moan escaping her lips, a sound that fuelled the fire within me.

Her hands then moved with a newfound boldness, exploring the contours of my chest. Her fingers traced the line of my collarbone, and the beat of my own heart quickened beneath her touch.

The unspoken desire hung heavy in the air, a tangible force drawing us closer. Without a word, I swept her into my arms, the lightness of her body surprising against the fierce intensity of our connection. She wrapped her legs around my waist, her body moulding against mine as if we were two halves of a whole, finally coming together.

Carrying her felt natural, an instinctive act driven by the overwhelming need to be closer. I took a few steps, the soft thud of our bare feet against the floor the only sound in the room. Our eyes remained locked, the unspoken promises and desires swirling between us.

I carried her; I reached the bed. The soft yielding of the mattress beneath us as we fell together was a final surrender. Our mouths crashed together, a desperate, hungry claiming. Hands roamed freely, seeking, and finding skin slick with heat.

Her breath came in ragged gasps, mirroring my own. The world narrowed to the feel of her against me, the scent of her skin, the taste of her mouth. Every touch was electric, igniting a fire that had been simmering for too long.

The rhythm between us intensified, a primal dance of pure sensation. Ayesha's body moved against mine with an urgency that mirrored my desperate need. Sounds of pleasure, soft moans, and gasps filled the small space.

The tension coiled tighter and tighter, a shared breath, racing hearts, the world dissolving into a kaleidoscope of feeling. And then, the shattering release. A wave of pure sensation washed over us, a moment of exquisite oblivion where nothing else existed but the two of us, finally, completely entwined.

As I was getting ready the following day, Ayesha approached me quietly. "I love you," she confessed, her voice soft, and sincere. "I want you in my life. I don't care about the age difference."

A playful smile touched her lips as she watched me dress. "You know, David," she teased, her eyes sparkling, "for a man in his forties, you possess a remarkable… stamina."

I met her gaze, a knowing smile curving my lips. “Ah, Ayesha,” I replied, my voice low and intimate, as I stepped closer. “A man’s strength isn’t just in youthful exuberance. It’s in the experience, the knowing... the ability to truly appreciate and pleasure a woman like you.” I leaned in and brushed a soft kiss against her temple.

Her emotions still held a certain weight, but my convictions remained firm. For me, ‘Sex’ and ‘Love’ occupied different realms; sharing intimacy was one thing, but the deeper connection of love was something else entirely. Our shared history and love transcending the physical intertwined my life with Nancy’s. That was why, even without a sexual relationship with Nancy, my heart remained tethered to her. My wife was my life, and I couldn’t dismantle that for the intensity of a fleeting encounter.

‘Sex’ was a craving I sometimes indulged in, a flavour my wife didn’t offer. I enjoyed the experience, but I ensured it remained separate; it was a pleasure not to be carried back into my life with Nancy.

As I was about to express my thoughts to Ayesha, she gently touched my lips, a knowing look in her eyes suggesting she sensed my internal struggle. “I’ll wait for you in the lobby,” she murmured, a hint of sadness in her tone.

When she left the room, a sense of unease settled within me. Had the intimacy we shared given her a false impression of my feelings? I got ready and entered the hall, waiting for our group to depart. We gathered our bags and began to move towards the cars.

As I got into the vehicle, Ayesha walked up to say goodbye. She turned to me, her eyes searching mine, a flicker of hope in her voice.

“Will you call me, David? I’d like to see you again.”

I took a deep breath, the weight of my decision settling upon me. “Ayesha,” I said gently but firmly, “please do not call or message me. My wife... she checks my phone."

"Wife." The word landed like a playful little bomb. Ayesha's eyes went wide, the light in them momentarily extinguished. Oops. She hadn't been expecting that particular plot twist. The realization struck her, altering our dynamics, a shift that didn't perturb me. I leaned in, my lips grazing her soft plum cheek, a lingering touch that conveyed what words couldn't.

I couldn't resist. I gave Ayesha a wink—half regretful, half mischievous—and climbed into my car.

A sly grin played on my lips as the engine roared to life. At forty, perhaps I was too old for such escapades, but a hint of recklessness never hurt anyone. It was a fleeting indulgence, a physical need met, nothing more.

But love? That was still something only Nancy could have.

The Maid

Last summer, Tina hired a maid to help us refurbish our house. Unfortunately, the agency placed us on a waiting list for a full-time maid. However, there were plenty of options available for part-time maids. I preferred a part-time maid, while Tina was more inclined toward a full-time one. Perhaps it's just how women are—seeking assistance from the moment they wake up until they go to bed at night. Eventually, I managed to convince Tina to hire a part-time maid. We had the financial means to support it and lived in a prominent, stylish neighbourhood in one of London's finest suburbs.

One day, Tina shared her struggle to find reliable help around the house with a neighbour. The neighbour immediately recommended Sharon, a woman who had worked for them and had proven herself to be diligent and trustworthy. Grateful for the recommendation, Tina contacted Sharon to see if she was available for work.

After their first meeting, Tina was impressed by Sharon's professionalism and work ethic. She felt reassured by Sharon's reliability, and she decided to hire her.

As time went on, Tina got to know Sharon better and discovered that she was not only hard-working but also kind, dependable, and always willing to go the extra mile. Sharon quickly became an indispensable part of the household, and Tina often wondered how she would manage without her. Her kindness made everyone feel warm and welcome.

Sharon began her new role the following week, taking on various household tasks. Her primary responsibilities included keeping the house tidy, making the beds, cooking meals, and maintaining the garden by pulling out weeds. However, she didn't limit herself to just these tasks. On weekends, when the household was busier, she did additional chores, such as ironing clothes, and accompanying Tina to the supermarket for supplies. Despite the increased workload, Sharon managed everything easily, consistently going above and beyond to ensure the household remained comfortable and happy.

One afternoon, I poured myself a glass of wine in the kitchen and glanced out the window. I saw Sharon working in the backyard. The oppressive summer heat made her sweat heavily, and I felt a pang of guilt for her enduring such harsh conditions—something I hadn't fully appreciated while in my comfort zone.

As I watched Sharon sitting under the scorching sun, I grew concerned that she might feel lightheaded. I decided to offer her something refreshing to drink. Without wasting time, I grabbed a pitcher of cold water and sliced a few fresh lemons. The invigorating combination of the lemons' tangy scent and the coolness of the water felt like a burst of energy, the perfect remedy to beat the oppressive heat.

I reached for a glass, the cool weight grounding me momentarily. My gaze drifted back to the window, and I noticed Sharon was no longer weeding; she stood still in the yard, her head turning slowly as her eyes scanned the perimeter with an intensity that suggested she was searching for unseen observers. A prickle of unease ran down my spine. Her behaviour felt odd and almost secretive, igniting my sudden, and intense curiosity.

As I peered through the kitchen curtains, my curiosity was piqued as I watched Sharon. She moved with grace and purpose, each gesture deliberate, and measured. With a sudden flourish, she removed her dress, and cast it aside, revealing a slender frame clad in a delicate white sleeveless top. The fabric hugged her curves, accentuating every contour of her body. The moment I saw her, her mesmerizing beauty captured my attention. I lost myself in admiration, momentarily entranced by her stunning appearance and unable to tear my gaze away from her. Her beauty was so captivating that I stood there in deep appreciation for a moment.

The way the sunlight caught the sheen of sweat on her youthful skin, tracing the delicate lines of her form beneath the white fabric, sent a jolt of something unfamiliar through me. It had been a long time since I had seen someone like this, and a long-dormant curiosity stirred within me. A warmth spread through me, a subtle arousal taking root as I continued to watch. I have been married to Tina for thirty years and have never been with anyone else. However, I have been curious about what it would be like to be intimate with someone else, and those thoughts have resurfaced today. I observed a young woman working outside in the sun for around ten minutes from my window. The sweat that ran down her cleavage ran in rivulets through each beautiful curve of her hips, accentuating her gorgeous body.

Confession: My feelings got aroused.

Tina entered the kitchen, curious about what had captured my attention. I quickly regained my composure and expressed concern for the girl outside, stating that I planned to offer her some water.

"Well, take it to her right away. I don't want her dying in my garden," Tina responded sternly.

I held a pitcher filled with chilled water and a bowl of freshly sliced mangoes as I stepped out of the house. Sharon stood in front of me with her back turned. Even though she was facing away, it was impossible to ignore her beauty. The contours of her back and the curves of her hips were as captivating as her face. With the sun shining down on her, she looked like a magnificent work of art.

I quietly stood behind her momentarily, taking in her alluring, musky scent. The aroma of a woman perspiring while working with her body is intoxicating. I could have stood there for hours.

Leaning closer, I let her musky scent fill my nostrils, and an impulsive thought took over. Lowering my voice to a soft murmur near her ear, I said, "That sun is relentless, isn't it?"

Startled, she turned and jumped into the air, knocking the jug of water from my hands and soaking me in the process.

Sharon's face turned pale with fear, her wide eyes filled with genuine worry that the spilt water might cost her the job she valued.

Her voice trembling slightly, she blurted out, "Oh, Mr. Roy, I am so sorry! Did I... did I get you wet?"

I lowered my sleek black Ray-Ban sunglasses, my gaze softening as I met her anxious expression. A small, reassuring smile touched my lips.

"It's quite alright, Sharon," I said gently.

A hint of mischief entered my voice as I added, my eyes lingering on her damp inner layer, "Though you have absolutely no idea…"

I couldn't help but notice the subtle flush that crept up her neck and bloomed across her cheeks at my remark—a delicate response that somehow amplified her youthful innocence. Despite my attempts to remain detached, I felt an undeniable pull towards her, a fascination as compelling as a moth to a flame. Her natural radiance was simply captivating.

The sun beat down on the patio, and a sudden thirst caught in my throat. I met Sharon's gaze and asked if she wanted something to drink. When she requested water, I gestured towards the patio table.

"There's more water over there, Sharon. Help yourself."

As she walked away, the gentle sway of her hips—a natural rhythm in her stride—caught my attention, stirring a subtle warmth within me. I felt a fleeting awareness of her gaze lingering on my back as I headed inside, silently acknowledging the charged air between us.

Later that night, as I lay in bed, the image of Sharon lingered in my mind—her youthful energy, the unconscious grace of her movements. It had been a long time since such a vivid impression had taken root, and my attraction was becoming increasingly difficult to ignore.

The soft rustle of fabric announced Tina's arrival. Her long black nightgown flowed around her like a shadow. The woman I had fallen in love with stood before me for a fleeting moment, and a flicker of hope stirred within my chest.

"Wow," I said, sitting up, my voice carrying a genuine note of appreciation. "You look stunning tonight, Tina."

She offered a tired smile, her eyes barely meeting mine. "Thanks. It's been a long day, Roy."

I reached out, my fingers lightly brushing against her hand. "Maybe we could just be together for a while? It feels like it's been too long."

She sighed and gently pulled her hand away. "Not tonight, please. Your mother called again. She's being utterly impossible."

A sense of longing washed over me.

"I just miss us, Tina. I miss you."

She walked over to the dresser and picked up her overnight bag.

"We'll talk when I get back from Rishi's wedding. I need some air, some space... this house feels heavy lately."

The next morning, sunlight streamed through the window, but the heaviness from the night before still lingered. I stepped outside, seeking solace in the garden. The vibrant colours of the blooming flowers against the clear sky usually brought me peace, but today, my fascination with Sharon drew me out. I had always found Sharon's quiet dedication to her gardening fascinating. She was a vision among the flowers—like a fairy come to life. The way she cared for each bloom with such devotion, then ran after butterflies with the joy of a child… I couldn't look away.

Wearing my favourite shorts, I caught my reflection in the glass door. A quick flicker of self-consciousness mixed with pride at the results of my gym efforts. The freedom of being shirtless felt familiar, and I indulged in a quick flex of my bicep. Age might be catching up with me, but I refused to let it diminish my feelings.

As I stepped onto the patio, the sun's warmth enveloped me. The air hummed with the buzzing of bees and the gentle rustling of the leaves. I set down my wine glass and reached for the sunscreen; the citrusy scent reminded me of carefree days. The familiar ritual began—slow, circular strokes across my chest and arms. When I reached behind my back, my fingers fell short, unable to cover that awkward middle spot.

That's when I saw her. Sharon stood near the rose bushes, her simple sundress swaying gently in the light breeze, a wide-brimmed hat shading her face, a watering can in hand. There was an effortless grace in her movements.

"Hey, Sharon!" I called out casually. "Could you lend me a hand with something?"

She looked up, a hint of uncertainty crossing her face. "Yes... Sir?"

I offered a relaxed smile. "You can drop the 'sir,' Sharon. Just help me with some sunscreen? My back's not cooperating today."

A moment of hesitation flickered across her face as her hand paused with the bottle. "Of course," she murmured, her voice barely audible.

I turned and sat forward on the chaise lounge to give her access. For a moment, the only sound was the distant chirping of birds.

"You still there?" I asked playfully, glancing back.

A nervous laugh escaped her. "Yes—sorry. The cap was being a little stubborn."

I felt the fabulous squeeze of the bottle, followed by an unexpectedly generous dollop of lotion spreading across my back.

"Oops! I think I overdid it," she said, a flustered note in her voice.

I chuckled and glanced back with a smile. "You think?"

She grabbed a nearby towel, dabbing away some excess before her touch settled onto my back. Her movements started cautiously but gradually became slow and surprisingly gentle, infused with quiet tenderness as she spread the lotion.

For a fleeting moment, the awareness of her nearness transcended mere attraction. There was a different kind of connection in the shared silence, under the sun's warmth, as something unspoken passed between us.

After expressing my gratitude towards Sharon for her help, I settled into the comfortable sunbed and gazed in her direction. As I basked in the sun's warmth, I couldn't help but notice her captivating presence and the way she moved with such grace. Her mere presence had an inexplicable effect on me, igniting a feeling of excitement and anticipation within me.

That night, as I lay in bed, I suddenly realized how lonely

I was. I had been alone for so long that I had become numb to it, but that night, the weight of my solitude hit me. Even when Tina was physically beside me, her mind was always elsewhere, lost in the blue glow of her phone screen. She would be glued to her device, scrolling mindlessly through social media, leaving me to my own devices. I thought I had grown accustomed to the emptiness, but something within me changed that night. A sense of unease settled in, indicating that the carefully constructed walls around my loneliness were beginning to crumble.

The usual remedies – a solitary glass of wine and a shower's numbing coolness – offered no solace. The silence in the house felt less like peace and more like a suffocating absence. I yearned for a genuine connection, a shared glance that acknowledged my existence, a voice that truly heard me before I felt entirely adrift. But alas, I was alone in my thoughts and feelings, with no one to turn to.

The following day, Tina, the only elderly member of her family, informed me that she would stay at her brother's place for the next two nights. I understood and appreciated her role as an elder, especially considering the motherly role she had taken on for her brother.

The aroma of freshly brewed coffee filled the air as I sat at the kitchen table, trying to dispel the overwhelming feelings of anger, loneliness, and stress that had burdened me since I woke up. I sipped the hot liquid, hoping it would soothe my nerves, but it didn't offer much relief. Just then, I noticed Sharon outside, working on the porch. She was tending to her plants, watering them, and pruning the overgrown leaves. I watched her from the window, feeling a sense of comfort and warmth. Seeing her so focused and serene made me forget my troubles, if only for a moment.

After a few minutes, she looked up, and caught my gaze. I waved hello, feeling shy, but she smiled back at me, her eyes crinkling at the corners. It was a small gesture—a simple upturn of her lips and the warmth in her eyes. Still, in the quiet ache of my solitude, it felt like a lifeline, a momentary acknowledgement that I wasn't entirely invisible.

Saturday settled in with an eerie stillness; Tina's absence echoed through the empty halls. I knew I needed to pay Sharon for her third week of work. Before I could call her, she appeared at the door of my study, her voice polite as she informed me she had finished her tasks and was ready to leave.

"Just give me a few minutes to get your payment, Sharon," I said, turning from my desk.

As she waited, I sensed her hesitant movements through the house, a quiet curiosity guiding her steps. Truthfully, a part of me had hoped for this.

Then came a soft knock on my bedroom door, followed by her gentle, slightly nervous voice. "Mr. Roy? Are you in there?"

When I opened the door, the towel knotted loosely around my waist, a subtle warmth spread through me, and I felt a feeling of... anticipation.

The moment Sharon's eyes registered where she had inadvertently found me, a deep blush bloomed on her cheeks.

"Oh! I... I'm so sorry, Mr. Roy," she stammered, her gaze dropping quickly.

"I can come back tomorrow for the payment."

I offered a reassuring smile.

"Nonsense, Sharon. It's alright. Come in, have a seat." I gestured towards the edge of the bed.

She hesitated momentarily, then stepped inside, perching herself on the very edge of the mattress, her posture stiff, her hands clasped tightly in her lap. Her brown eyes darted around the room, avoiding mine with an almost palpable nervousness.

I moved a little closer, observing her discomfort.

"Am I making you nervous, Sharon?" I asked, my voice low, and steady.

She bit her lip, a brief flicker of indecision crossing her face before she nodded almost imperceptibly. "A little," she admitted, her voice barely a whisper.

"You... you make me feel a bit shy. Awkward."

Her gaze remained fixed on the ceiling, her fingers twisting together in her lap. But then, her eyes flickered down to me, a fleeting glance before she whispered, "Sometimes... I catch myself looking at you." A deeper flush stained her cheeks. "And sometimes... it doesn't feel quite right."

Intrigued by her hesitant admission, I leaned forward slightly.

"Doesn't feel right? What do you mean by that, Sharon?" Her reaction, with nervous energy radiating from her, stirred something within me—a subtle sense of influence.

"Well," she began, her voice a little shaky, "it's just that... you're very... strong. I mean, I've never really noticed... a man like you before." Beads of perspiration dotted her forehead.

"You're... attractive," she added, her voice softening almost to a breath, "and sometimes... It's hard to look away."

Spending time with her made me increasingly aware of her innocence and a certain sweetness she possessed. A long-dormant instinct began to stir within me, a feeling of wanting to… care for her. Perhaps it was the subtle signs of vulnerability. I sensed it—whether it was the quiet itself or the contrast to Tina's growing distance, I couldn't tell. But whatever it was, a protective impulse had begun to take root.

I walked towards her slowly, stopping just a few feet away.

Gently, I lifted a finger, and lightly touched the underside of her chin, tilting her gaze towards mine.

"There's no need to be nervous around me, Sharon," I said, my voice carrying a low, almost flirtatious tone.

A small, hesitant smile touched her lips, and the blush on her cheeks deepened.

"Tell me a little about yourself, Sharon," I asked, softening my tone.

"Your family, what you enjoy doing... what makes you happy."

As she began to speak, her voice still a little shaky, I moved to the small bar cart and poured myself a glass of wine, the clinking of the glass the only other sound in the room.

"Do you... have much experience with relationships? With... men and women?"

Sharon's hands tightened further in her lap, and I noticed a subtle shift in her posture, a slight guarding of her chest. Her breathing seemed a little shallower.

"Have you... have you ever been with a man... intimately, Sharon?" I asked, my voice dropping to a more probing level.

A flicker of something akin to offence crossed her features, quickly replaced by a renewed nervousness.

"No... sir," she replied, her voice a little louder than a whisper, her gaze darting away.

"But... I have seen... pictures."

I leaned against the wall behind me, deliberately shifting my posture, letting my muscles flex subtly beneath the towel. Sharon's eyes flickered down my body, a quick, almost involuntary glance before returning to somewhere over my shoulder.

"Would you like to see?" I asked softly, lifting my right hand to graze my bicep casually.

Although Sharon remained silent, her wide eyes held a mixture of apprehension and a flicker of something unreadable. I moved closer, the air between us charged with an unspoken tension. Her gaze flickered down, her breath catching slightly. I took her hands, her skin surprisingly soft, and gently placed them on the taut muscles of my shoulders. A subtle tremor ran through her fingers. Her gaze lifted to mine, a silent question in their depths.

"You can touch, Sharon," I murmured, my voice low, sensing the curiosity that radiated from her.

"I know you're curious."

My hand found the nape of her neck, my thumb lightly stroking the sensitive skin there, a subtle invitation.

The contrast of her smooth hands against my skin was stark and strangely intimate. As I subtly shifted, guiding her hands lower towards the curve of my back, I felt the almost imperceptible tightening of her grip.

Her hesitant touch ignited a response within me, a primal stirring I hadn't anticipated. I felt a subtle shift in her breathing, a delicate flutter against my chest as her nearness intensified. My own body responded, a silent testament to the pull she exerted. My glance slipped downward, a quiet admission of our physical reality.

Sharon looked up at me, her eyes holding a vulnerability that tugged at something within me.

"Could I... could I see?" she whispered, the question barely audible.

Without a word, I took her hands once more, guiding them slowly towards the edge of the towel that clung to my hips. My breath hitched slightly as I let her touch linger there for a fleeting moment, the anticipation building. She fixed her gaze on the point of contact, a mixture of apprehension, and intense curiosity on her face.

Eventually, I eased the towel downwards with a slow deliberation that felt charged with unspoken meaning. The whisper of the fabric falling to the floor amplified the silence in the room. I stood before her, exposed, allowing Sharon's gaze to take in the entirety of me. A soft gasp escaped her lips, her eyes widening with a look that held both surprise and a dawning awareness. I retook her hand, my touch firm yet gentle, and placed it briefly on my thigh, silently acknowledging our unspoken desires.

Moving closer, the warmth of her skin radiated towards me. My hands found the delicate curve of her shoulders, my thumbs tracing the soft line of her collarbone. A subtle tremor ran through her. Gently, I cupped her face, my eyes locked with hers. The air thrummed with a silent energy.

With a slow, deliberate motion, I reached behind her, and unfastened the clasp of her skirt, letting it slide silently to the floor. My gaze then lowered to the delicate line of her thigh.

The air between us still thrummed with unspoken possibility.

"Thank you, Sharon," I whispered, warming my breath against her skin.

I saw the dawning awareness in her eyes, the newness of the sensations she was experiencing. There was no need to rush. I extended the envelope, a silent promise of perhaps... more later.

A strange mix of emotions flickered across her face—lingering curiosity, a hint of surprise, and perhaps a dawning understanding of the unspoken boundaries.

In the days that followed, a subtle shift occurred in our dynamic. When Tina was home, our interactions remained polite but minimal, consisting of fleeting exchanges of glances. However, in Tina's absence, an undeniable undercurrent remained. Sharon began leaving a single, beautiful flower on my desk each morning, a silent offering that carried a weight of unspoken communication.

I remember sitting on the porch with Tina one afternoon. While she was engrossed in a phone call, her attention was miles away, and Sharon worked quietly in the nearby garden. A casual hand would settle low on my abdomen, the subtle pressure against my belt a direct, unspoken request. Sharon's gaze followed the touch, a pulse quickening in her throat as a flush stained her skin, and then a shy, almost hesitant smile touched her lips.

Her responses became bolder, too. A lingering touch as she handed me a tool, her skirt riding a little higher on her thigh as she bent to dust. Once, as she passed, her fingers grazed the neckline of her blouse, a deliberate adjustment that offered a tantalizing glimpse of the shadowed valley between her breasts. The constant threat of discovery and the nearness of Tina's rooms away infused these moments with a raw, exhilarating tension.

Weeks blurred into a tapestry of stolen glances and subtle provocations, each encounter pushing the boundaries of propriety. The higher the risk, the more intensely our awareness of each other sharpened.

One morning, the unexpected quiet of the house greeted me. Tina was gone. An idea, both reckless, and irresistible, took root. I found Sharon in the kitchen.

"Sharon," I said, my voice casual, "could you bring the bath towels to my room? I seem to have misplaced them."

A knowing smile flickered across her lips, a silent acknowledgement of the shift in the atmosphere.

"Of course," she replied, her eyes holding a hint of anticipation.

"I'll be up in a few minutes," I caught Sharon's eye as she worked, a fleeting acknowledgement that held a spark of something illicit.

The humid air hung heavy as Sharon pushed open the bathroom door, a cloud of steam momentarily obscuring her silhouette. I leaned against the cool porcelain of the sink, the dampness clinging to the thin fabric of my underwear.

"There's a fresh towel behind you," she murmured, her voice a little husky as she stepped closer.

Her gaze flickered over me, a silent acknowledgement of the intimacy of the setting before she leaned in, and her lips brushed mine—a soft, tentative touch that held a question.

"Perhaps," I replied, my breath warm against her ear, "you should shed that dress and let the steam embrace you instead."

My eyes drifted down the length of her, a silent invitation.

With a slow deliberation, her fingers found the buttons of her dress. The whisper of fabric filled the steamy air as it slid from her shoulders, revealing the delicate curve of her skin. Our gazes locked, an unspoken language passed between us before our lips met again, this time with a deepening intensity, a shared exploration of taste and breath.

My hands found the warmth of her back, the slickness of the water droplets clinging to her skin beneath my touch. I drew her closer, the soft yielding of her body against mine igniting a slow burn within me. Her hands moved, tracing the line of my jaw, a feather-light touch that sent shivers dancing across my skin. The closeness was a silent promise, a heightening of desires in the confined space.

The thought of Tina's potential return pulsed beneath the surface of our awareness, adding a dangerous thrill to the moment. Driven by an impulse, I lifted Sharon by the waist, her legs instinctively wrapping around me as I placed her on the cool countertop. Her fingernails pressed into the nape of my neck, a silent language of anticipation as I moved against her.

The mirror behind us vibrated subtly against the wall, reflecting our entwined forms in the hazy steam. Our movements became more urgent, a silent rhythm building towards a crescendo of sensation. A low groan escaped my lips, a surrender to the overwhelming pleasure as the world narrowed to the feel of Sharon's love around me.

Just then, the distinct click of the front door unlocking echoed through the tense silence. A sharp intake of breath escaped Sharon's lips. She clung to me for a fleeting moment, silently acknowledging the near discovery. Then, with a swiftness born of adrenaline, she gathered her discarded clothes and slipped out of the bathroom, a ghost disappearing into the steam-filled air. The house held its breath, the intoxicating thrill of our shared secret lingering in the silence.

One weekend afternoon, Tina was watching a show in the living room; she called Sharon over to the kitchen to help me open a jar. The moment Sharon stepped in, the tension between us surged. I pulled her close and kissed her with an urgency that had been building for days. My hands found her curves, and she responded, her lips tracing mine with equal hunger. She explored my body with familiar affection, sensing my growing desire.

As soon as we slipped into the bedroom, our passion ignited. I took Sharon in my arms, our bodies moving in perfect sync, driven by need, and reckless emotion. Every touch, every moan felt amplified by the thrill of secrecy. The warmth of her skin against mine, the rhythm of our passion—it was overwhelming. There was something animalistic in our union and yet something intensely emotional, almost desperate.

Tina remained in the living room, unaware, and it felt like time had stopped for us for a moment. We lost ourselves in each other's touch—lips searching, hands wandering.

But that fragile illusion shattered when Tina decided to take a nap and came searching for me. She opened the bedroom door, only to find Sharon's legs around my waist and my hands tangled in her blouse.

The world seemed to tilt on its axis. This was it; everything was about to shatter.

Tina's scream sliced through the air. In the chaos that followed, she lunged at Sharon, her fury uncontrollable. Her hands flew in a flurry, hitting, shoving, and screaming. At first, Sharon stood her ground, stunned, and overwhelmed. Then, suddenly, Tina turned to me, and slapped me hard.

That was the breaking point.

Sharon's eyes widened, her chest rising, and falling with rage and heartbreak. The woman who had remained silent through Tina's blows was no longer calm. She stepped forward, trembling—not with fear but with fury born out of love. She grabbed a heavy metal sculpture from the nearby table in an instant and raised it above her head. Her grip was tight, her jaw clenched, her body shaking.

It wasn't about revenge—it was about *me*.

"Sharon, stop!" I shouted, my voice cracking, terrified of what she might do.

She froze for a second, her eyes locked onto mine—pain, betrayal, and something even more profound—an aching, desperate love.

Everything was spiralling. Tina was trembling and sobbing on the floor. Sharon, panting, mascara streaked down her cheeks. And me—frozen, guilt-ridden, lost.

Tina's voice cracked as she screamed, "Get out! If I ever see your face again… I swear I'll kill you!"

Sharon, shaken, reached toward Tina in a gesture of remorse, but Tina shrank away. I stood still, helpless, the weight of my choices collapsing around me.

After a tense silence, Sharon turned to me, her eyes filled with concern. She gently took my hand, her voice soft, and gentle. "Are you okay?"

My throat tightened. I couldn't speak. "Please… just go," I whispered, the words a desperate attempt to shield Sharon from Tina's rage, even as a part of me crumbled.

Her eyes welled with tears. "You don't mean that."

But I did. I needed space to breathe, understand, and heal what had fallen apart.

"You're only making it harder," I whispered. "I'm okay… but you have to leave."

Tina was still sobbing behind me, cursing under her breath. Sharon looked at me one last time, her eyes shimmering with love and sorrow. She kissed my hand, then turned, and walked away.

And my heart shattered.

After a challenging period for me and Tina, things gradually returned to normal in our household. However, despite the progress, I still felt lost, and alone. I dealt with the pain of losing so much while Tina struggled with her anger.

Then, one afternoon, while I was home alone, I heard a faint knock at the door. Curious, I opened it.

No one was there.

I stepped outside and looked both ways—nothing.

But just as I turned back, I saw it.

And then, a single white flower on the ground caught my eye.

The same kind Sharon used to place on my desk.

I stared at it, stunned. Was it a coincidence? A memory? Or was it… her?

Whatever it meant, that simple bloom gave me something I hadn't felt in a long time.

Hope.

Lockdown Romance

As a writer, my life has been a tapestry of stories, characters, and the comforting presence of my loyal dog. I'm also a devoted husband, sharing my days with my wife, Nikita, who is a passionate teacher. Her dedication often extends her school hours to six days a week and sometimes even more.

I make it a point not to work on weekends, hoping to spend those precious hours with her. However, she often has plans with friends. Loneliness has many shades; the quiet hum of the refrigerator can sometimes feel like its soundtrack. But when that silence is handed to you by the person you love, it echoes with a more profound emptiness.

Today, a memory tugged at me as I sat sipping coffee and watching the sun struggle through the clouds. A bittersweet invitation landed in my inbox: the London Literary Festival. That city holds a part of my past. It has given me joy, creativity, and a secret I've never dared to share.

Three years ago, I embarked on a rare solo journey—a week immersed in the company of fellow writers. 'The London Literary Festival' was a grand celebration of literature, vibrant with the promise of new connections. I recall the exhilaration of being alive and the anticipation of meeting kindred spirits worldwide.

One meeting would leave a lasting impression on my soul amidst the crowd and the buzz of conversations.

Her name was Lavina. She was striking—a woman in her forties and an Indian author like me. I first spotted her across the room, dressed in a bright yellow sari that caught the light with every graceful movement. Her silver bracelet chimed with a delicate rhythm as she signed books for eager readers. Her jet-black hair, styled in an elegant bun, caught the soft glow of the spotlight, highlighting her features with a quiet intensity.

She wasn't just a woman but a character who came to life.

We writers often exist between our real lives and the stories we imagine. Sometimes, the lines between the two blur. As I stood there, I realized I was already weaving her into the fabric of my next novel.

I'm not sure how long I watched her, lost in thought and creating a world around her in my head, until someone tapped my shoulder for a selfie, pulling me back to the bustling reality of the book fair.

When I saw her again, a subtle current of anticipation stirred within me. I scanned the crowded hall, searching for her. I finally spotted her conversing with Ranjit, one of my co-writers. Without thinking, I started moving in their direction, a casual trajectory that would bring me within earshot. I offered Ranjit a brief nod as I passed, a silent signal of acknowledgement, and as expected, his eyes followed me.

"Hey!" Ranjit called out, waving me over.

I turned back with a casual smile, trying to appear to have noticed them. As I joined their small circle, Lavina turned to me, her smile an easy, genuine curve that immediately eased the lingering hum of the crowd.

"I'm Lavina," she said, extending her hand, her silver bracelet chiming softly.

I took her hand, the warmth of her touch surprisingly grounding amidst the fair's energy.

"It's a pleasure to meet you. I've heard of your work."

"That's rare," she chuckled, her eyes crinkling at the corners. "Most people are far too polite to admit they haven't."

A shared laugh eased the initial formality between us.

I learned she was married and a mother of two, having flown in for the festival just like I had—yet her presence radiated youthful charm and quick wit that instantly drew me in. Our conversation flowed effortlessly, touching on the shared joys and frustrations of writing, the chaotic world of publishing, and those small, insightful observations that make up the fabric of life.

I found myself gravitating toward her company for the remainder of the day. The connection felt easy and engaging, punctuated by shared laughter that built an invisible bridge between us, warming the air around us. As the day drew to a close, we exchanged contact numbers—a casual agreement to stay in touch and a silent promise of a connection that felt too significant to let fade.

We intended to leave the following evening, but everything shifted suddenly, and unexpectedly. The Ministry of Education announced the cancellation of all literary events. News reports of airport closures began to circulate. London, it seemed, was bracing for a strict lockdown...

The coronavirus variant spread rapidly across large areas of the United Kingdom, creating a chaotic atmosphere. I had rented an apartment for a few days near the River Thames. The beauty of the Thames and the empty roads added a sense of tranquillity to my solitude.

While reflecting on Lavina amidst the lockdown chaos, a genuine concern ignited within me, stronger than mere camaraderie. I reached for my phone, needing to ensure her safety.

When she answered, I could hear the tremor of anxiety in her voice—understandable, given the situation—and a decision formed instantly. I drove to the location mentioned and found her near a silent, shuttered bookstore. She glanced around the deserted street, clutching her phone like a lifeline, her eyes darting with unease.

As my car pulled alongside the curb, I noticed the tension in her shoulders begin to ease.

"Thank God," she breathed, a whisper of relief escaping her lips as I stepped out.

"Are you alright?" I asked, my concern genuine.

"I've been calling everywhere," she replied, her voice tight.

"No one is taking guests. It's… unsettling out here."

"I figured," I said, locking eyes with her for a moment in silent acknowledgement of our shared uncertainty.

"Come stay at my place, Lavina. I have space. It's... quieter there."

A slight furrow appeared on her brow. "I don't want to impose."

"You're not," I assured her, managing a small smile. "Look, I'm just a writer who makes decent coffee and has a spare room with a view of the Thames."

A faint smile returned to her lips, providing a brief respite from her worries.

"You're incorrigible."

"And occasionally right," I responded, motioning towards the car. "Come on."

As we pulled up to the apartment, Lavina felt a wave of relief visible in the way her tense shoulders relaxed. The sight of the familiar building brought her a sense of safety and comfort.

Once inside, Lavina surveyed the peaceful space.

"This place... it has a good energy," she murmured.

"The view helps," I replied, nodding toward the window

where the River Thames shimmered under the muted light.

She walked over to the window, inhaling deeply, a sense of calm settling over her.

"It's strange. It doesn't feel like lockdown here. Just... a pause in the noise."

My smile softened.

"There's a room right next to mine. Choose whichever you prefer. You'll be comfortable."

"Thank you," she said, her eyes meeting mine, a silent acknowledgement of more than just shelter. "This...this kindness means more than you know."

In the stillness of the apartment, we shared a quiet understanding.

"Sometimes," I said softly, "a little quiet is all that feels real in all the chaos." Lavina nodded in agreement, her eyes reflecting the shared sentiment.

She offered a grateful nod and moved toward the spare room.

I stepped into the living room, the city lights beginning to bleed into the twilight beyond the window. I pressed my phone to my ear.

"Hey," I said, my voice low.

"Are you alright?" Nikita's concern was apparent.

"I saw the news... London's in complete lockdown?"

"Yeah," I replied, trying to keep my tone even.

"Everything's cancelled. Airports are a mess. I've rented a place near the Thames. It's quiet."

"You're alone?" There was a sharp note of inquiry in her voice.

I hesitated for a moment. "No... a couple of writer friends are around. We're staying close, just in case," I said, forcing a light chuckle that felt hollow even to my ears. "You know, trying not to lose it."

She exhaled slowly. "I wish you could just come back. This makes me anxious."

"I know. I'll figure something out soon," I reassured Nikita, a knot of guilt tightening in my chest. "Don't worry about me. Just take care, okay?"

"Okay," she murmured, a hint of longing in her tone. "Miss you."

"Miss you too."

I ended the call, the weight of the unspoken truth settling heavily in the quiet room. The city outside, once vibrant, now felt like a silent witness to my carefully constructed lie.

After the call ended, I stared blankly at the screen, a quiet ache settling in my chest. Why did I lie? The weight of guilt and uncertainty pressed down on me like a heavy fog that refused to lift.

I told myself it was to protect her—to spare her the unnecessary worry, the overthinking, the imagined scenarios. But was that the real reason?

Or was it something else?

A flicker of guilt crept in. Was I lying for my wife's sake or my own?

I tried to shake the thought off, but it lingered like the scent of her vanilla perfume in the hallway. No matter how I justified it, one thing was clear: I lied.

And the truth was… I didn't fully know why.

After the call, I saw Lavina stepping out of her room. Her hair was still damp from a shower, and she smelled faintly of vanilla and jasmine. There was something comforting about her presence, something so soft, and graceful that it almost felt unreal. For a moment, I stood still, watching her—not with desire, but with a strange sense of closeness, as if the sudden stillness of the world outside bound us together.

Suddenly, her phone rang—it was her husband. Respecting her privacy, I gave her a slight nod and quietly stepped into the kitchen. From where I stood, I could still hear the softness in her voice as she spoke.

"No, don't worry... I'm somewhere safe," Lavina said gently, then paused. "No, not a hotel. Just... a private place."

Her words were simple, but they left something unspoken, like mine. I leaned against the counter, letting the moment settle in. Both of us had chosen silence over detail. But why? Was it a form of protection, guilt, or something else we didn't yet understand? That unspoken truth hung between us like a delicate but real thread.

Smiling at the coincidence, I poured two cups of coffee and returned to the living room. As I handed her one, Lavina's fingers brushed against mine—just briefly—and it was enough to stir something inside me that I wasn't ready to name.

We both spoke about our families back in India and our ideas about future work. We got so lost in conversation that we didn't notice how the evening melted into the night. It felt like talking to an old friend and a new one simultaneously, sharing our experiences, and finding common ground.

I was astonished—I've never been talkative, not even with my wife. But with Lavina, it was different. There was an ease, a connection that deepened with every word. She was full of stories and life. I discovered she was a brilliant writer and a mind-blowing chef. She smiled as she promised to cook something special for me the next day.

As we returned to our rooms, we turned simultaneously and said softly, "Good night."

The next morning, I woke up to the aroma of cardamom tea and Spanish omelettes. I checked the time—it was 7 a.m. I could hear the clanging of pots and the humming of the coffee machine. I quickly freshened up and walked out.

The breakfast table was a delightful spread. Lavina had prepared various dishes, and seeing them made my appetite roar. She stood by the kitchen counter, wearing a long, breezy dress, her damp hair cascading down her back like silky strands. She looked like a fresh lily in full bloom.

"I hope you're hungry," she chirped, brushing a strand of hair behind her ear.

"I'm starving," I replied, smiling. "And I feel fortunate."

We spent the day watching movies, catching up on the news, and talking endlessly. There was no awkwardness, no gaps to fill. We spoke to our spouses once a day, keeping our conversations light, and omitting the fact that we were not alone.

While laughing over tea, Lavina said, "I haven't laughed this much in years."

"Neither have I".

Lavina shared stories from her youth that had us both laughing out loud. But later, there was a quiet moment when her voice softened.

"Eighteen years of marriage," she said, looking down at her half-empty mug. "We're good friends, but… sometimes, I feel invisible." I nodded in understanding. "I get it. It's like the world assumes you're happy because you're married. But inside, there's this emptiness."

Our shared feelings of loneliness created a bond of empathy between us.

She looked at me, not surprised, but seen.

That emotional connection between us only grew stronger.

We spent five days together. Despite our closeness, we never crossed any boundaries. We respected the lines set by our marriages, but those lines began to blur in moments of silence and glances that lingered just a second too long.

Then, on the sixth day, Ranjit called.

"You'll be flying back tomorrow. All systems are back on," Ranjit said.

When we heard the news, we had to leave the next day, both of us looked devastated. Spending so many days together had made us feel like we had much to share and discuss.

Lavina and I exchanged glances. That call should have been a relief, but instead, it felt like saying goodbye too soon. We had somehow forgotten about the world outside our apartment.

As I packed my suitcase that evening, I noticed Lavina standing alone on the balcony, gazing out at the Thames.

I stepped out beside her. For the first time, I truly saw the river. The city lights danced on its surface like scattered diamonds. There was a softness in the air that hadn't been there before—or perhaps I had never noticed it until now.

"I don't want to go back," she whispered.

"Me neither," I replied without thinking.

She turned to face me. The breeze played with a strand of her hair, and gently, I tucked it behind her ear.

Her eyes searched mine. There were no words, just emotions—unspoken yet undeniable.

I wrapped my arms around her, and she melted into my chest like she had been waiting for that embrace her whole life. Time stood still; nothing mattered except the warmth between us.

When we kissed, it wasn't driven by lust but rather by longing, connection, and something that had quietly and intensely grown between us.

We both returned indoors, the air thick with unspoken yearning. Our kiss deepened, becoming a desperate exploration that tasted of shared moments and the bittersweet knowledge of their impending end. My hands, trembling slightly, traced the delicate curve of her neck, the warmth of her skin beneath my fingertips igniting a slow, burning sensation within me. She responded to my touch with a soft sigh, her hands finding their way to the small of my back, pulling me closer until there was no space between us.

Shedding her clothes felt like unwrapping a precious gift; each revealed an inch of skin, a testament to the beauty I had come to cherish in our brief time together. Her form was soft and yielding, the gentle swell of her breasts and the curve of her hips fitting perfectly against my touch. A shared breath escaped our lips as our naked bodies finally met, the sensation of skin on skin sending a wave of both ecstasy and a profound sense of connection through me. We clung to each other, lost in the silent language of touch, the moment's urgency tempered by an underlying tenderness.

Our lovemaking wasn't a frantic release but a slow, deliberate exploration of the intimacy we had carefully guarded. The weight of our shared experience imbued each kiss and caress, a silent conversation spoken through touch. The joining felt like a natural culmination, a merging of not just bodies but of the unspoken emotions that had bloomed in the quiet of the lockdown. She accepted me with a grace that mirrored the depth of her heart, her soft moans a testament to the pleasure we found in this forbidden closeness.

Afterwards, we lay entwined, the silence filled with the gentle rhythm of our breathing. Lavina's head rested on my chest, the soft weight a comforting anchor. Her fingers traced invisible patterns on my arm, each stroke a lingering echo of our shared intimacy.

"I'm not sure what this was," she whispered, her voice still thick with emotion.

"Neither am I," I replied, husky, "but in this strange, suspended moment, I wouldn't trade it for anything."

When we finally succumbed to our yearning, it transcended mere physicality. It was a profound reawakening of emotion, a surge of warmth, and vitality that had lain dormant for years. It served as a stark revelation of the emotional terrain I had unwittingly inhabited.

After a beautiful night together, we had to part ways. Our time together illuminated a truth: soulmates aren't always the ones we marry but those with whom we forge a deeper connection. Some couples are fortunate to spend their lives with their soulmates, but the connection may come from unexpected places for others.

Lavina entered my life recently, leaving an indelible mark in just a few days. Despite my long marriage to Nikita and our shared life journey, she hasn't stirred my soul in the same way.

Saying farewell to Lavina felt like a quiet severing, a poignant end to a vibrant interlude. I followed the rules, stepped into my car, and drove away, leaving some of myself behind in that London apartment.

A week later, I received a familiar buzz on my phone, signalling a message from her:

Lavina: *"I just walked past that little café we loved. I swear I heard your laugh."*

Me: *"I was thinking about that exact spot today."*

That simple exchange sparked a fragile ember of joy, reminding me of our shared, unexpected intimacy. Soon, our messages became a cherished ritual—whispered words across the digital divide during the quiet hours after her husband left for work. We exchanged recipes, book ideas, and small worries; these virtual conversations became a lifeline during the grey expanse of lockdown, a secret garden where I felt truly seen.

As weeks turned into months, the familiar chime of her messages became a rare melody. Each unanswered notification felt like a tiny door closing. A hollow ache settled in my chest when she mentioned her family vacation. It wasn't exactly jealousy but rather a profound sense of absence—the silence where her quick wit and understanding used to reside. These days, the stolen moments of her evening walks were the only threads connecting us, fragile lifelines in a sea of my quiet contemplation.

Then, the inevitable message appeared on my screen:

Lavina: *"Hi… I'm back."*

Me: *"I'm glad."*

When her voice finally came through, it carried a distant happiness, a contentment that resonated with her return to her established life. A sharp pang of loss echoed in my chest at the thought of her turning to her husband, enjoying the intimacy we had briefly shared. It felt like a quiet closing of a door I hadn't realized I'd hoped would remain open. As a writer, I could imagine countless scenarios, but the reality of life moving on—and her moving on—held a quiet finality. The sense of loss was palpable, a wound that refused to heal.

Now, our calls serve as quiet reminders of what we once shared. Lavina speaks of her husband with a renewed warmth that I celebrate outwardly, offering genuine—if slightly weighted—congratulations. Beneath each cheerful word lingers a bittersweet ache, silent mourning for the 'what could have been' that now feels forever out of reach. This one-sided connection leaves behind a quiet sense of helplessness that I carry long after the call ends.

When her text finally came today, the familiar irritation I had felt due to our dwindling contact vanished, replaced by a wave of relief and a deep empathy for the delicate balance she was trying to maintain.

"Thinking of you," Lavina said.

My heart fluttered involuntarily—a mix of relief, a sharp pang of nostalgia, and a yearning I couldn't quite identify. My fingers hovered over the keyboard as I typed slowly:

"And you. Always."

The words hung on the screen, a final echo of a connection forged in extraordinary times. As I looked at them, a wave of resolve washed over me. This lingering tether, however poignant, was a barrier to the future I now envisioned—a future rooted in the home I had almost lost. With a deep breath, I selected her contact information and tapped 'Block User.' The digital severance felt stark, absolute. A quiet sadness settled in its wake, but beneath it was a sense of finality and a necessary closing chapter. This closure was not just a choice but a necessity for my future.

Setting the phone down, the weight of our unspoken goodbye settled around me like a shroud. In the ensuing silence, the question I had been avoiding finally emerged: Can I continue to exist in these fragmented spaces of connection and separation?

The answer remained elusive. However, the lockdown had unearthed a profound truth: I was capable of feelings I had almost forgotten, of truly being seen. If I could rekindle that spark, it wouldn't be too late to bring it home to Nikita. The thought of failing, of things not working out with my wife, got a familiar ache, but it wouldn't shatter me. I had tasted aliveness again. The depth of my feelings surprised me, a revelation I couldn't ignore.

That evening, I sat beside Nikita in the living room. She looked up from her book, a flicker of surprise in her eyes at the unusual softness in my gaze.

"Can we talk?" I asked, my voice thick with vulnerability I hadn't allowed myself to show in years.

It was a moment of raw honesty, a courage I hadn't felt in a long time. "I've been thinking... about us. About what I've missed."

The weight of my words hung in the air, a testament to the courage it takes to confront one's emotions.

Tears welled in her eyes, mirroring the raw honesty in my own. "I want that too," she whispered, her voice trembling.

At that moment, a fragile understanding took root. Love wasn't just a sudden spark—it was a quiet, daily choice, like caring for a shared garden. The isolation of COVID-19 had shaken our world, but maybe it had also made space for something new. I felt a stirring—an urge to show more affection, to face the cracks we'd ignored, and to be open again to the love I once overlooked. As night fell, a soft, unfamiliar peace settled over me—a small but steady hope for a future I hadn't dared to dream of just weeks ago, a future that held growth potential even in the face of adversity.

The Unscripted Life

I am Ashraf, a retired man from the motion picture industry. In my youth, the roar of the camera, the sudden hush before "Action!", and the frantic energy of a movie set coursed through me like electricity. I moved from one project to the next, each new role a jolt that made me feel vividly alive. I played many character roles—some on the big screen and others on television—always alongside the stars, but never quite one myself. Nevertheless, I was known, respected, and even loved in the industry.

I was never a man of formal education; school never held much interest for me. However, cinema became my classroom, my textbook, and my temple. I would spend hours watching legendary actors, absorbing their styles, and expressions. I copied their hairstyles, the way they walked and talked, and even the way they smiled. I wasn't born an actor; I became one. Acting wasn't just my job; it was the fire in my blood, the only language my soul understood.

When my family began to worry about my future and the instability of my unconventional jobs, my elder brother offered me guidance.

"Ashraf, stop chasing shadows. Go where the lights are—films might not make you rich, but they'll keep your soul fed."

I took his advice. Through a few fortunate meetings and connections with small-time suppliers, I found steady work. It was a struggle to survive at first, but with perseverance, and hard work, I eventually thrived. This journey from mere survival to thriving is a testament to the possibilities of life.

Marriage came as a formality rather than a desire. I wasn't ready to settle down, but some decisions are made for you in our world. My wife, Nargis, came from a deeply conservative family, a world that was a stark contrast to mine—quiet, obedient, and steeped in traditions. She was a good woman, dependable, and kind in her way. If I ever tried to share a playful wink across the dinner table, her gaze would remain steady, perhaps even a bit bewildered, as if I had spoken in a foreign tongue. She wasn't the type to flirt or laugh out loud, nor the kind to dance with me under the stars. These cultural differences added a layer of intrigue to our relationship.

Back then, I had imagined marriage as an endless stream of romantic touches in the hallway, whispered jokes, and stolen kisses. However, with the birth of our second child, the romance began to fade.

"I'm tired," she'd say, pulling away when I reached out. "The children need me more."

As my days filled with work, my nights turned into a cycle of cries and changing diapers. My home no longer echoed with love; instead, the rustle of her prayer beads, the children's muffled arguments behind closed doors, and the heavy silence between us marked it. I remember reaching for her hand on the sofa, craving a moment of silent connection. But she gently pulled away to adjust the pleats of her sari—a small act that somehow felt like a softly closed door. Our marriage had become a silent film, filled with expressions but lacking sound and genuine communication.

Surrounded by the allure of beautiful women on set, the charm of good company, and the glamour of stunning locations, I appeared to live a fairy-tale life, at least on the outside. I was admired, envied, and even desired. However, inside, a void began to widen, creating a stark contrast to the external admiration I received.

Nargis felt like a tightly shut window on a stormy night—no matter how loudly my heart knocked, the warmth never came through. I longed for an emotional connection, for the feeling of being truly seen and valued.

When the affection from Nargis stopped coming, I sought warmth elsewhere. Not out of lust, but in search of that feeling I thought I'd lost forever: the simple acknowledgement in a woman's eyes, the easy laughter in response to a story—a reminder that people still saw me, still valued me, something my own home rarely offered.

Initially, I worked only one shift daily—either in the morning or the evening. However, as time went on, I began accepting double shifts. It wasn't about the money; it was quieter on set than at home.

"Sunday is ours," I told Nargis one day while she was chopping coriander for her siblings' lunch, trying to maintain her gaze.

Without missing a beat, she replied, "Sunday is family day. They're coming over by noon. Can you pick up some ice cream?"

I took the keys and dropped the idea of ever asking her again.

My children immersed themselves in their tuition, friends, and sleepovers worlds. Although the house was bustling with their activities, it felt emotionally muted. Family dinners had become silent affairs, interrupted only by requests for salt or the clinking of cutlery. Nargis focused on serving while I concentrated on finishing my meal. Our sons ate quickly, eager to return to their television shows—a subtle reflection of the lack of warmth or connection that could have brought us closer together. Nargis floated through the rooms like a guest burdened with responsibilities. When I spoke, she nodded, and when I touched her hand, she instinctively moved it to adjust her dupatta. I longed for a deeper, more meaningful connection, but it seemed to elude me.

Over time, she became more of a tradition than a woman I loved. Her affection felt measured in teaspoons of salt rather than in moments of eye contact. This lack of love and warmth inflicted a great deal of pain on me. Wives often think their husbands are always hungry for food, but why can't they realize there's more to life than just meals? This emotional void was a constant source of struggle for me.

So when Pappu, my supplier, called me about a ten-day outdoor shoot in Ooty, I quickly packed my bags before the conversation ended. I didn't leave a note on the fridge. I looked forward to the trip, enjoying the company of my friends and the production crew. It was a fun experience, and the payment was reasonable. The prospect of being away from home, even for a short while, brought a sense of relief and escape.

'Ooty' provided me with the space to breathe again. Laughter felt different in the hills—lighter, more youthful. The cameras rolled, the crew teased, and the nights were warm, wrapping us in a comforting embrace. So were the smiles of the women who asked how I was doing, laughed at my stories, and didn't mention gas cylinders or spiritual fasts.

But the shoot ended—as all escapes do—and I found myself back in the familiar silence of home.

Back home, Nargis returned to her prayer beads and sermons. She invited me to join her at the shrine to walk barefoot and pray for peace.

"I'm still alive, Nargis," I snapped one time. "Let me live now. You fast for the afterlife, but I'm hungry for the present."

During that time, I had numerous affairs with women. There were so many passing faces and fleeting nights—each stolen moment offered temporary relief from the persistent ache of loneliness. In their eyes, I saw a reflection of the man I used to be—the man Nargis no longer seemed to recognize. Yet, even in those brief connections, I remained aware of the emptiness; I understood that these encounters were not the deep, lasting affection I truly craved.

I enjoyed my life and stopped waiting for love and affection from my wife. Nargis had become a ritual—a daily routine served on steel plates, spiced with complaints, and garnished with silence. She was happy with her social gatherings and often acted like a fighter cock, always ready with a bag of grievances.

I won't lie—I wandered. I wasn't counting the women; instead, I was counting the stolen glances and whispered compliments—those moments when I felt genuinely seen and desired, not just a fixture in a family portrait. My youth returned not as a distant memory, but as a rebellion against the invisibility I felt at home—a primal need to reclaim the feeling of being wanted, the spark that had once made me feel alive and vital.

When smartphones became common, I experienced a brief sense of pleasure; suddenly, the world, and its fleeting secrets were within my reach. I dove into the digital landscape, spending days exploring social media like a novice rediscovering a long-lost playground. The likes and comments on my carefully curated photos echoed the applause I once craved—a fleeting sense of relevance in a world that increasingly felt like it was moving on without me. I knew it was shallow validation, but it offered a welcome distraction nonetheless. It was as if I had discovered a new world where I could be anyone I wanted to be and temporarily forget my loneliness.

The women I interacted with were from different continents, their temporary attention serving as a fleeting balm for my persistent loneliness. Late-night chats became my refuge, often stretching past two in the morning. Nargis's earlier, milder complaints had faded into a distant murmur that I largely ignored. Meanwhile, she had become increasingly devoted to her spirituality, with her days filled with fasting and visits to distant shrines—our paths diverging further with each passing year.

The night the dam finally broke, her voice overflowed with years of unspoken frustration. "Turn off that cursed phone, Ashraf! Stop acting like a teenager clinging to a fading fantasy. Don't you feel a sliver of shame? Look at yourself—hunched over that glowing screen all day, applying ridiculous filters to your tired face! Trying to project that grand hero image to strangers, huh? Uploading those smoothed-over selfies as if you're still the young buck on the studio lot! But the truth, Ashraf? Look in the mirror! Those wrinkles on your face could tell more stories than your old film reels, deeper than the creases in my finest silk after the monsoon. And that thinning white hair? It's practically waving a white flag! Any day now, it'll all abandon you, leaving you bald, and staring into the abyss of your vanity. Shame, Ashraf! Shame!"

For a fleeting second, I thought I saw a glint of hurt in her eyes before they hardened into a familiar anger. Her scorn ignited a fire in me, a desperate need to defend the last vestiges of my perceived vitality. That night, I roared louder than intended in response to her accusations about my phone and selfies.

"Shame on me? At least I'm not praying my desires into oblivion! At least I'm honest about the emptiness I feel in this… this silent mausoleum we call a marriage! I don't care, Nargis, alright? You immerse yourself in your spiritual circles and endless gossip with those pious old women—leave me to find my solace. I spent my youth as a background actor in my own life, waiting for a spotlight that never found me. Thanks to this phone and this digital world, I get to write my script, even if it's just one fleeting scene at a time. So, for once, just… stay away."

"Oh, I'm sure," she snapped, rolling her eyes with theatrical disdain.

"When you finally shuffle off this mortal coil, all this nonsense—your pathetic late-night flirting, those ridiculous photo filters, your entire double life—will personally escort you straight to the gates of Jannah! Maybe they'll even roll out a red carpet for the great digital Hero!"

"Jealous, you old crow?" I retorted, puffing out my chest in a pathetic imitation of my younger self.

"These wrinkles still get more attention online than your endless 'Chilla' updates and your pious selfies at the shrines! Even my grey hair has more followers than your hundred forwarded WhatsApp sermons!"

That night, we retreated to separate rooms, the silence between us thick and palpable. Not for the first time. Not, I suspected, for the last. The finality of our separation hung in the air, a heavy shroud over our strained relationship.

I became a master of duality, purchasing two smartphones—one pristine white for fulfilling family obligations, the other sleek black, a portal to my after-hours indulgences. On the white phone, I meticulously curated the image of the ideal patriarch. I posted religious quotes on my WhatsApp daily with clockwork piety. My replies to family queries were prompt and laced with concern—a digital halo I polished with practised ease. I often imagined my relatives saw me with one foot already on the celestial staircase. It was a game of control and perception, and I had become a master of it.

But the black phone? That was my secret garden—its screen blooming with forbidden fruit, sweetened by whispered intimacies. Late-night video calls glowed with stolen smiles, flirty texts danced across the glass, and virtual giggles echoed into the quiet darkness. To my surprise, the women on the other end were scattered across the globe, many of them wearing wedding rings, just like Nargis, and me. The difference lay in their hunger, not for polite small talk or spiritual salvation, but for a flicker of desire, a spark long forgotten by their ageing husbands. They craved to feel seen again. And Nargis? My wife was no exception.

Strangely, guilt never came knocking. Or if it did, it stood quietly outside, waiting for an invitation I never sent.

And there I was—retired, the embers of my youthful energy still glowing faintly, and improbably, a reluctant messiah for this clandestine club of neglected wives. Who would have ever cast me in that role? It was a role I never imagined, a part I never auditioned for, yet here I was, playing it with a sense of disbelief and self-reflection.

It was a bitter irony that the bright faces on that small screen showed more genuine curiosity about the mundane details of my day than the woman who lay beside me in the quiet darkness of our shared bedroom. Her silence was a chasm, a void that echoed without connection.

Whenever Nargis found solace in her world of prayer and pious gatherings, I slipped away into the clandestine glow of my other life. In that digital sanctuary, women offered fleeting attention but genuine curiosity, whispered secrets, and sometimes, the vulnerable intimacy of shared images. The thrill we exchanged became a shared currency—a silent understanding transcending mere physicality.

Let's be honest: a mutual hunger drew us together.

If the woman who shared my name had warmed the quiet ache in my chest and the cold expanse of our bed, this elaborate deception might never have taken root. But human hearts—whether male or female—aren't sterile vessels. They crave warmth.

The reassurance of a touch.

The validating whisper that someone still desires them.

The bitter truth that society often overlooks is the emptiness that frequently precedes infidelity. We judge the act, not the gnawing void that drives it—left untended for too long, unmet needs become desperate architects, carving paths to escape. These women, each trapped in her silence, found a reflection of their loneliness in mine. Some even suggested, with a boldness born of desperation, that once their husbands retreated to their obligations, a "friendly visit for some sugar" could be more than a neighbourly gesture. I don't recall the drink we shared, but I distinctly felt the stir of long-dormant embers.

In their company, something unusual happened. The weight of fifty-five years seemed to lift, occasionally replaced by a fleeting memory of being thirty-five and sometimes even the spirit of being twenty-five. I casually told Nargis I would meet "old friends," a technically truthful but somewhat distorted version of reality. After all, some of them had a wealth of experience, having lived through significant life events and gained the wisdom that comes with age.

We navigated these encounters with a silent understanding, a mutual agreement to avoid the complicated mess of romance or heartfelt declarations. We were two adults recognizing a basic human need, providing each other with a form of mutual, no-strings-attached comfort. Yet, every so often, a faint whisper of discomfort would arise—a fleeting awareness that this carefully crafted balance might be more fragile than I was willing to admit, highlighting the intricate nature of adult relationships.

While browsing through various apps, new faces would appear, each representing a fleeting connection. Beauty, I found, is an expansive landscape. What truly captured my attention was the initial spark of intrigue, the candid honesty in their messages, and the raw acknowledgement of our shared yearning, fostering a sense of connection.

One silent night, my fingers tapped on the phone screen as I scrolled through my social media feed with the habitual ease of routine. It was just another evening lost in the digital tide when a friend request appeared from a name I didn't immediately recognize: Noor—a nineteen-year-old girl from Kashmir. My scrolling came to a halt. Her profile picture caught my attention; her smile exuded a disarming warmth, and her eyes sparkled with youthful curiosity.

Her posts showcased a vibrant tapestry of Kashmir's breathtaking landscapes. I noticed she returned the gesture as I tapped the 'like' button on a few of her photos. This interaction was brief and innocent, a simple exchange of appreciation for each other's posts. Yet, something about Noor stayed with me—her vibrant energy and effortless charm. Soon, our exchanges became comments, shared jokes, and friendly messages.

"You're so funny!" Noor replied quickly, her enthusiasm apparent in her message.

"Your dancing videos always make me smile."

A smirk crossed my lips as I texted back. "I'm glad to hear that! Just trying to keep humour alive in this chaotic world, Noor. You know," I continued, a new thought striking me, "you remind me of the younger version of myself. We should catch up sometime."

My regular conversations began with Noor, a science student from Kashmir, who often shared photos that vividly captured the stunning scenery around her. I was increasingly drawn to her youthful energy and found it hard to resist complimenting her beauty. As our interactions continued, a fragile yet real connection started to form across the digital divide.

Several months passed, and what started as harmless banter gradually, almost imperceptibly, became more intimate. Despite my better judgement, I became increasingly drawn to Noor's persistent flirtation and the intoxicating attention she showered on me. On her part, Noor appeared to develop genuine feelings for me—feelings that began to significantly influence our digital exchanges.

One evening, as I balanced conversations with various online acquaintances, a message from Noor buzzed on my phone, sending a jolt of anticipation through me. The image she sent revealed her in a provocative pose, clearly meant to catch my attention.

"How do you like this one, Ashraf? Just for you," the text read.

My eyes widened, my breath catching in my throat. "Wow... Noor, you're something else."

Her youthful figure was undeniably captivating, and despite my efforts to stay composed, a flood of forbidden thoughts surged through me. As time passed, our conversations grew more intimate, with Noor gradually sharing more revealing pictures and videos, each one pulling me deeper into the allure of our secret connection.

Staring at the latest image on my phone, I muttered to myself, a conflict brewing within me. "God... She's irresistible. What am I doing?"

With each passing week, my flirtation with Noor intensified. She became more insistent and demanding. However, this shift carried an unexpected burden—her increasing possessiveness. Initially, it appeared as just a few scattered messages throughout the day, but soon, her name began to dominate my notifications. I couldn't unlock my phone without her digital presence demanding my attention.

A message from her arrived early, cheerful yet undeniably demanding. "Good morning, Ashraf! I've been waiting for you to wake up. Are you ready to talk all day?"

I smiled strainedly. Whenever I saw Noor's name, a subtle suffocation crept in. "Morning, Noor. I've got a lot of work to get done today, but I'll text you later."

But Noor's persistence didn't waver. A sad emoji appeared almost immediately, followed by another desperate text. "Don't you miss me? I feel like we can't go a day without talking."

My heart began to pound with unease, and frustration tightened its grip. "Look, Noor, I'm not saying I don't enjoy talking to you, but I have a life and a family. I can't be on my phone all day."

Her response was swift, a digital plea: "I just want to be with you, Ashraf. You're the only one I talk to. Can't we spend more time together?"

A heavy sigh escaped me as I stared at the screen, the weight of the situation pressing down on me. "I don't know, Noor. This feels... like too much."

One evening, I felt my eyes narrow in frustration. Noor didn't understand what I was going through, and I could not clarify my confusion or resolve her feelings. I realized I needed to end this before it became even more complicated.

My fingers hovered over the phone screen, and my stomach twisted in knots. The weight of the decision I faced was overwhelming; my heart pounded in my ears, and my hands shook. I had been here before, caught between the life I had built and the allure of something forbidden. But now, as I stared at Noor's desperate pleas, something shifted within me. It wasn't just panic or guilt; I recognized a troubling pattern.

I reflected on my boredom at home, my craving for validation, and my habit of chasing fleeting connections instead of facing the deeper issues in myself and my marriage. I saw how my unmet needs had led me here, not just hurting Nargis emotionally but possibly causing real pain to a young woman who mistook my loneliness for love. That realization marked a painful step in self-discovery I could no longer avoid.

A wave of shame washed over me—sharper, more profound than the guilt I was used to. I wasn't the vibrant, desired man I pretended to be online. I was a man escaping his life, grasping at quick fixes while ignoring the quiet decay of a long-term commitment. Noor's infatuation held up a mirror to my desperation, and the reflection was anything but flattering.

Taking a deep, shaky breath, I didn't just decide to end things with Noor. I made a different choice—one rooted in self-preservation and a growing awareness of my broken patterns. My fingers hovered above the screen, not to block her but to write a final message. One that, while rejecting her, carried a belated honesty—perhaps the first true thing I'd offered in a long time.

I typed, "Noor, please listen to me. You're young and deserve real love, not this... this fantasy we've created. I'm married, and I need to focus on my own life and responsibilities. What we have isn't real, and it's not fair to you. I'm not the man you want. I have to end this, for both of our sakes."

After sending that message, I finally blocked her number, which felt heavier, and more consequential than just cutting off contact.

I stared at the phone for a long moment, my mind no longer numb but filled with unsettling self-awareness. The question of whether blocking Noor was the right choice still lingered, but now it was accompanied by a deeper question: What will I do about myself? This introspection was a new and uncomfortable experience for me. I placed the phone face down on the table and exhaled deeply, sinking into the chair as the weight of my self-recognition crashed over me. The world felt still and quiet, but the storm inside me had taken on a different, more introspective form.

Six months have passed, and I haven't heard a single word from Noor—no calls, messages, or digital breadcrumbs leading back to her. It's as if she vanished into the digital ether.

Meanwhile, the landscape of my home remains stubbornly unchanged. Nargis remains devoted to her spirituality, her days marked by a gentle rhythm of prayer beads and meticulous planning for family gatherings. As for me? I've never felt more profoundly bored within the familiar walls of my own house.

The endless scroll of social media fills my evenings—fleeting connections still sought but now approached with cautious restraint. Most of my conversations are with married women; they are familiar with the unspoken rules of the game. There's no mess, no drama, no emotional strings. Just light conversation, a harmless flirtation, a shared fantasy whispered across the digital divide—and then, a quiet log-off, as if nothing of consequence had transpired.

Even the intimacy I once shared with Nargis feels like a fading photograph—blurred, distant, touched by time. It's not just age, though that too plays its role. It's the weight of routine, the unspoken silences stretching between two people who once breathed each other in easily.

Sometimes, I wonder why the bloom of romance begins to wilt when children arrive. It is as if the marriage certificate, once shadowed by a birth certificate, becomes a document of completion for them.

And that's when husbands like me begin to gaze out the window—not searching for someone objectively "better," but simply for someone who can make us feel visible again, desired again. Not extraordinary, just… a man again.

5 E

Some moments in life leave such a deep imprint that they become part of who we are—etched beneath our routines, whispering their memory even in silence. This story, a secret I carry quietly, continues to echo through my days, shaped by a single, unforgettable encounter.

Every day, my world revolves around the demanding yet fascinating corridors of a science centre in Hyderabad. My work calls for precision, presence, and an ever-curious mind. While my wife often finds a refreshing change of pace by visiting her parents in Mumbai, I rarely crave such interludes. For me, purpose lies in movement, in challenges met, and in a life lived with intention.

Last year…

The memory unfolds with a clarity that defies the passing of time. I had just boarded my flight home after presenting my research on gene therapy at a conference in New Delhi. The talk had been well-received—a gratifying conclusion to weeks of focused work—yet quiet fatigue clung to me, the kind that unfamiliar cities tend to leave behind. Mumbai called to me with its familiar rhythm, comforting noise, and the quiet intimacy of home that I had begun to crave more than I'd realized.

My thoughts drifted to my wife—the soft curve of her smile and the knowing warmth in her eyes. I recalled the comfortable silences we often shared, punctuated by gentle touches, and unspoken understandings. The anticipation of returning to that haven, to the simple pleasure of holding her close, was a soothing balm. It had been too long since our last shared intimacy. That tender dance of affection left us both feeling content and connected.

I thought about gently unwrapping the silken layers of her sari, revealing the delicate lingerie beneath—a whisper of the vibrant spirit she once wore so openly. I could almost hear the soft gasp that sometimes escaped her lips, feel how her hand would find mine in the dark, and taste the ache of a longing I hadn't known I'd been nursing. The need to return to the comforting familiarity of home grew urgent.

When the final passengers trickled onto the plane, a quiet hope stirred within me: perhaps the seat beside me would remain empty—a silent companion for a weary soul. But fate, as it often does, had a different narrative in mind.

I looked up as a tall, striking woman paused before my row, gracefully lifting her bag into the overhead compartment. The subtle contours of her figure, briefly accentuated by the motion, caught my eye, and something stirred inside me—a sudden, unexpected thrill—as the air shifted.

She settled into the adjacent seat, and our eyes met for a fleeting instant—a mere heartbeat in time, yet it carried a weight beyond its briefness. Immediately, she retrieved her laptop, exuding focused energy as her elegant fingers danced across the keyboard, navigating the silent language of emails. The rhythmic tapping of her keys resonated with the sudden quickening of my pulse, drawing me into an unexpected state of concentration.

What was it about this woman that so swiftly captured my attention, holding it fast in invisible threads?

My mind began weaving a tapestry of quiet speculation without a word exchanged. Perhaps she was a CEO or a driven entrepreneur who carved her path with precision, realizing her ambitions through sheer determination and quiet perseverance.

She appreciated the finer aspects of life, perhaps even those touched with a hint of the unconventional. Her confident, direct gaze conveyed an innate sense of authority, a quiet command in the professional sphere and perhaps beyond. Her finely sculpted lips held the subtle suggestion of a knowing smile, exuding confidence that hinted at a mastery of unspoken communication.

As I observed the delicate grace of her hands and the impeccable grooming of her nails, I sensed an understanding of the subtle power within a gentle touch—the ability to influence with understated finesse. Her captivating presence presented this; her form spoke of mindful care and attention. Her allure seemed to be a potent yet unspoken influence.

Twenty minutes into the flight, I found myself completely absorbed by the woman sitting next to me. The cabin was dimly lit, and the gentle hum of the plane's engines filled the air. I considered ordering a hot cup of tea and opening the book I had packed in my bag, thinking that might help me relax. However, I couldn't help but be distracted—my gaze kept drifting toward her, and the book remained shut on my lap.

It was probably just a fleeting infatuation, a harmless echo of schoolboy curiosity. I reassured myself that I would forget her as soon as we landed. After all, I was a reserved academic, not used to such spontaneous encounters.

She stayed focused on her laptop, eyes scanning what appeared to be a business contract, while her fingers glided effortlessly across the keyboard. At one point, she absentmindedly rubbed the top of her leg as she read, and although it was a simple motion, it stirred something within me.

Suddenly, she turned, and caught me looking.

Her lips curved into a playful grin. "See something interesting?" she asked, her tone teasing yet calm.

I felt heat rise to my cheeks. " I-uh, sorry," I muttered, fidgeting with the in-flight magazine. "I just... zoned out for a second."

She chuckled softly and shut down her laptop. "Long day?" she asked, reaching for her magazine.

"The longest," I replied, managing a smile. "I presented at a conference today on genre therapy."

"Interesting," she said, flipping a page with a slow, graceful motion. "I was in New York last week for a leadership summit. I picked this up there," she added, extending her wrist to show me a delicate bracelet.

"It's beautiful," I said, grateful for anything to focus on other than the growing warmth between us.

"It caught my eye. I'm drawn to things that aren't obvious," she said, her voice barely above a whisper.

I nodded, pretending to listen to the story she continued to share, but I wasn't truly paying attention. Her voice was soothing, but my senses were elsewhere.

Then it happened—her leg brushed against mine. The fabric of my trousers came into contact with her bare knee. She didn't move away, and neither did I.

She locked eyes with me again, calm, and collected.

"Comfortable enough?" she asked, a hint of mischief in her tone.

I held her gaze, my voice steady despite my racing heart.

"Very," I replied with a smile, "though you're making it hard to relax."

"Well," she said, tilting her head slightly, "some flights are meant to be remembered."

As I fumbled over my thoughts, she shifted the focus back to me and asked, her voice sweet as honey, "So, where are you flying tonight?"

Her tone wrapped around my spine like silk, both warm, and tingling. I wasn't a natural at flirting; small talk had never been my strong suit.

"Just heading home," I replied awkwardly. Then, without warning, I started rambling about a half-baked idea regarding behavioural patterns in scientific research. When I realized I was talking too much, she was already smiling politely, and I fell silent, feeling embarrassed.

Then, like a small girl, she leaned closer and, with a conspiratorial smirk, said, "Don't laugh, but I'm secretly a science nerd too. But shhh… It's our secret."

We both laughed—two grown-ups suddenly sounding like teenagers sharing secrets behind the school lab. The warmth of her breath lingered on my cheek longer than I'd like to admit. Her perfume—earthy and floral—hung between us, making the cabin feel a few degrees warmer. The soft hum of the plane's engines, the gentle vibration of the seat, and the subtle scent of her perfume all added to the surreal atmosphere.

She casually mentioned an article on global warming she had read that morning in *The Times of India*, but I couldn't focus. I just sat there, watching her lips move, imagining them brushing against the sensitive skin near my collarbone. It was impossible not to drift into my thoughts.

That's when it struck me. She wasn't just talking; she was hunting. I was no more than willing prey. She easily saw through my nervous charm and quiet distractions and knew exactly what to do with it.

I tried to recover by nervously starting another science

anecdote. But before I could get through the first sentence, she lifted a finger, and gently pressed it to my lips.

"Shhh," she whispered.

My breath hitched. The soft pad of her finger against my mouth was maddening. I struggled to resist the wild urge to lean in—just slightly—and taste that smooth skin.

Her touch trailed down slowly, teasing my chest, and grazing my thigh—deliberate yet feather-light.

Then she leaned in again, her voice low and velvety:

"Undo the top button of your shirt."

I obeyed, my heart racing. Emboldened, I reached for the following button, only to feel her hand halting mine.

"No," she whispered.

"Only what I say. Nothing more. Nothing less."

The dim cabin lights cast long shadows that danced to the gentle hum of the plane. A sea of reclined seats and closed eyes stretched before me. Even the soft murmur of the air hostess at the front felt distant, separated by the charged bubble forming around us. A strange thrill rose in my chest, a heightened awareness of possibility cloaked in the illusion of safety.

A fine sheen of perspiration slicked my skin, each drop tracing a slow path downwards. Her hand in mine felt like a live wire, sending a tremor of anticipation through me, a delicious weakness spreading through my limbs. The unspoken question of what lay ahead throbbed beneath the surface, growing stronger with each passing moment of the flight.

"Close your eyes," she murmured, her voice a silken command. I obeyed instantly, my other senses heightened in the darkness. A heat blossomed in my core, a primal urge to surrender to her will and let her take control.

"Let me lead tonight," she whispered in my ear.

Desire surged through me like a second heartbeat. Her tone had changed—it was no longer playful but authoritative. I was more than willing to yield.

In that exact hushed moment, she whispered something else: "Go. Wait for me."

I didn't ask where; I already knew.

I stood up, my movements feeling awkward under her intense gaze. As I turned to walk down the aisle, a strange awareness washed over me when my belt buckle brushed close to where she sat. I felt a phantom sensation of her breath, warm, and expectant, seem to move through the fabric of my trousers, and the air around me suddenly thickened with a palpable heat.

Each step down the narrow aisle felt heavy with the intensity of her gaze on my back. I slipped inside when I reached the lavatory; the latch clicked, sealing us in separate moments of anticipation. The silence that followed stretched on, each second amplifying the frantic beat of my heart as I waited.

My palms were sweaty, and my breath was uneven. Then, I heard the latch turn.

The door opened slowly, almost tantalizingly. She stepped inside, locked it behind her, and turned to face me.

We didn't speak.

There was no distance between us, only heat. Her hands found my chest and deliberately undid the top button of my shirt—not hurriedly, but like part of a ritual. I cupped her face and guided her mouth to mine as we kissed—deep, unrestrained, and hungry.

My trouser belt buckle clattered against the tiled floor, a slight sound swallowed by the rush in my ears, the frantic pounding mirroring the anticipation thrumming through me. My fingers fumbled with the zipper, the fabric whispering as it fell away.

Lifting her, my hands spanned her waist, the yielding warmth of her body pressed against mine, igniting a firestorm that consumed all thought. Each touch was a revelation—the smooth silk of her blouse against my chest, the bare heat of her skin beneath my seeking hands, a desperate exploration. Our heartbeats hammered in unison, a frantic rhythm mirroring the growing urgency of our movements—a slickness developed between us, a testament to the rising, almost unbearable heat. When my fingers found the clasp of her bra, her breast swelled into my hand, the soft weight a potent invitation, the faint scent of her desire rising to meet me. A primal urge took over, and my mouth closed over her nipple, a frantic, almost desperate claiming, the salty taste of her skin a raw connection. Reason dissolved, replaced by the slick friction of her skin against mine, the intoxicating scent of her desire filling my senses, her soft moan a helpless response.

Every motion, sigh, and brush of skin felt like a secret meant only for the night sky outside. It wasn't just desire; it was surrender—unapologetic, wild, and unforgettable. We remained in that tiny room, tangled, and breathless, long after the fire had dimmed. Neither of us spoke; we didn't need to. The silence conveyed everything.

A silent understanding passed between us as we began the slow, almost reluctant separation. Before she moved to leave, her hand found mine, pulling me close one last time. A tremor ran through me, a lingering echo of our fierce passion. She leaned in, her lips brushing softly against mine. It wasn't a kiss filled with hunger but one that held the promise of something deeper, something I could never have. For a moment, I closed my eyes, savouring the sweetness of her lips, trying to remember her scent, her warmth—everything about her. I knew I would never experience this again, not in this lifetime.

The sound of the lavatory door closing behind her amplified the sudden emptiness. In the mirror, a stranger stared back at me—hair dishevelled, with the top button of my shirt torn off, a stark reminder of what had just happened. I smoothed my hair and adjusted my collar, a futile attempt to erase the evidence of a moment that irrevocably changed me. A nervous hope flickered within me, wishing my outward normalcy would conceal the lingering tremor of excitement coursing beneath my skin. Thankfully, my coat offered a protective shield.

The pilot's announcement of our imminent arrival felt jarring, a sudden return to reality I wasn't quite ready for. Back in my seat, a wave of self-consciousness washed over me. I avoided the gaze of the passenger beside me, silently agreeing to the unspoken discomfort. As I closed my eyes against the dimming cabin lights, vivid memories flooded back—almost dreamlike yet undeniably real. The insistent thrum of my heart and the lingering sweetness on my lips were irrefutable proof of what had just happened.

When the plane taxied to a stop and the cabin began to stir with movement, she leaned in one last time, her breath a warm whisper against my ear—a final, fleeting touch that sent a shiver through me. I lingered on her, etching every curve, and nuance of her expression into my memory. With quiet grace, she gathered her belongings, and moved toward the exit.

Once she reached the door, she paused, and looked back at me. For a fleeting moment, our eyes met, and it felt as though the world around us stood still. I could sense everything she wanted to say in that instant, but never could. A smile tugged at the corner of her lips, almost as if she reassured me that this moment would remain with her.

Then, just as quickly as she had entered my life, she was gone. The door closed behind her, and life continued.

I sat there for a long moment, staring at the empty seat 5E—the place where everything had begun. It was just a number, a seat, but it reminded me of a moment that changed me forever. It was the seat where she sat, where we connected—where I learned that some connections are too brief to last but too deep to forget.

In some part of my heart, I would always carry the memory of her: the way her touch made me feel like I was falling, the way her eyes held a thousand unspoken words, and the way her presence left an indelible mark on my soul.

As I glanced out of the window, I took a deep breath, letting go of the ache in my chest. I knew that some stories are meant to be lived only in the heart. I would keep this one forever, just as she had kept seat 5E, a place forever tied to us and that unforgettable connection.

Maybe our paths will never cross again. Perhaps she was a dream that chose me for a night. But I know this: every time I fly, I book seat 5E—not for comfort, not for class—but in the hope that one day, she'll return to it.

The Unsigned Papers

The clinking of glasses and the low murmur of conversation in the bar barely register tonight. Sonam's absence presses down like a heavy weight, her silence echoing louder than the noise around me. Where her quick laugh once bloomed, there is only a void.

She left today.

The words loop in my mind, each syllable soaked in regret, deepening with every swallow of whiskey. Sonia's perfume still clings to my collar—the ghost of a morning embrace—sharp, intimate, cruel.

Knowing Neetu waits at home is a leaden ache. The thought of our shared bed feels unbearable now. That space beside me, once hers, is cold.

I ache to confess everything—the stolen moments, the source of this hollow that Neetu unknowingly fills. But the words stay trapped, a bitter lump in my throat. If only Sonam were here... her hand in mine, anchoring me through this storm of my own making.

About three months ago…

My name is Sumeet Singh, and I am 32 years old. I married Neetu in my twenties when we were both young and filled with naive certainty. We fell in love—or what we thought was love—and envisioned the comforting image of settling down together. At that time, we were genuinely happy with our decision, imagining a shared future filled with warmth and affection. However, as we matured, our understanding began to diverge, and a discordant tension replaced the easy harmony we had previously enjoyed.

"'Sex' and 'Passion'—the initial sweet delights of an immature love. However, responsibility acts like a pervasive salt, seasoning that sugary platter, and often overpowering its sweetness, leaving a residue of obligation. The relentless demands of work and the quiet erosion of family life have chipped away at the easy romance we once mistook for an unbreakable bond.

Every day, Neetu, and I found ourselves navigating a minefield of unspoken resentments, with our interactions frequently punctuated by arguments and blame. We both secretly wished to split up, yet the fear of exposing our fractured reality to our family kept us tethered. In front of them, we carefully played the roles of a happy, understanding married couple, a charade that earned us their constant admiration.

Once, my burdens grew too heavy to carry alone, and I hesitantly opened up to someone I trusted. The words clung to my tongue like a forbidden fruit—bittersweet, tempting, yet laced with fear. I often yearned to confide in friends, to seek the balm of their advice. But the fear of judgement, of unravelling the carefully woven illusion I'd lived within, kept me silent.

Perhaps it was cowardice. Maybe it was just the exhaustion of facing another storm.

Walking down a familiar street, I saw a sign advertising counselling sessions with Dr Kapoor, available for a manageable thirty minutes. It felt like an unexpected stroke of luck, a lifeline thrown into my internal storm, and I quickly made an appointment for the following day. It was a moment of hope amidst my turmoil, a sign that help was within reach.

The next day, when I visited Dr. Kapoor, he was already

waiting for me in his quiet office, a notebook, and pen in hand, the tip of the pen poised above the page. He looked up with a friendly smile that crinkled the corners of his eyes, introduced himself, and gestured for me to follow him into his counselling room. He was a 50-year-old man, bald, and short, with kind eyes magnified by round glasses. His presence immediately instilled a deep sense of trust and calm, a reassurance that I was in good hands.

As I entered his room, the city's cacophony faded away. Sunlight streamed through the window, illuminating dust motes dancing in the still air, creating a palpable sense of positivity in the bright space. A round glass coffee table and two white chairs stood before a large aquarium that bubbled silently. It was the first time I would attempt to truly open my heart and articulate the tangled mess within me to another person. The room's ambience eased the knot in my stomach, and I answered Dr Kapoor's initial questions with unexpected candour.

I spoke freely about the chasm that had opened between the "before" and "after" of my marriage, revealing all the unforeseen consequences of a love built on youthful idealism. My demanding work schedule, along with the growing list of reasons I had become emotionally distant from my wife, all tumbled out in detail—a torrent of unspoken truths finally finding release.

Dr. Kapoor listened patiently, his gaze steady, and unwavering. However, I couldn't help but wonder if he truly understood the depth of my discontent beneath the surface of my seemingly "normal" marriage. At the end of our session, he suggested another meeting for the following day, indicating that he wanted to grasp the scope of my situation fully.

That night, I slept peacefully, feeling a lightness I hadn't experienced in months. I couldn't fully understand what subtle shift in perspective Dr. Kapoor had triggered. At the dinner table for the first time, I registered Neetu's voice as she recounted the details of her day—the concerns about her mother's health, a minor issue at her workplace—the usual "blah, blah" that had turned into background noise. But this time, I listened without the familiar urge to interrupt or dismiss her.

After leaving my office the following evening, I ran into Dr. Kapoor, a sense of anticipation guiding my steps. He seemed to expect my arrival, and we settled into the consultation room. I didn't say much this time; the relief of feeling heard from the previous day still lingered. Dr. Kapoor remained patient and nonjudgmental. He grinned, a knowing crinkle appearing around his eyes as he addressed me by name while flipping through a few pages.

"Mr. Singh, I've thoroughly reviewed your information, and I'm pleased to report that your married life is perfectly normal."

Dr. Kapoor continued, a knowing smile on his lips as he observed my initial surprise, perhaps even a flicker of disbelief. "What you're experiencing—the friction with your wife, the frustrations, and the feeling of being overwhelmed by work and responsibilities impacting your personal life—are common challenges in long-term relationships. Marriage isn't always a smooth journey; it often involves periods of adjustment and re-evaluation. While considering drastic measures like separation might feel like an escape, I believe it's worth exploring the possibility of a fresh start. Reducing some of the pressure you're under could be a good first step. Have you thought about delegating some of your workload? Perhaps hiring an assistant could free up some of your time and mental space."

A surge of energy coursed through me as I listened, and a fragile seed of hope began to take root. I decided to take Dr.

Kapoor's advice—a desperate gamble, perhaps, to reignite the buried embers of romance in our lives.

The demands of architectural creativity often felt overwhelming, casting a shadow over my evenings. However, when Sonam joined as my secretary, a subtle shift occurred; a lightness began to permeate the usually stifling atmosphere of my office. Lifting the burden of administrative tasks released not only my schedule but also provided me with mental clarity. I started to leave the office at a reasonable hour, allowing me to enjoy the quiet of our home. The persistent tension with Neetu seemed to fade, replaced by a fragile calm—a truce rather than genuine peace. There were even a few nights when a hint of our earlier intimacy returned, echoing a connection I wasn't certain I still possessed.

Sonam was young, intelligent, and possessed a striking beauty that didn't go unnoticed, a subtle awareness sparking in my periphery from the moment she walked in. Professionally, she was exceptional, anticipating my needs, and managing my schedule with seamless efficiency. Sonam was always the first to arrive at the office and the last to leave, her dedication mirroring my ambition. Within a few months, her understanding of my work had become so intuitive that she could handle client communications with remarkable skill and insight, leaving me feeling supported professionally and subtly valued, in a way that my interactions at home no longer provided.

As the days passed, Sonam's presence in the office became a quiet anchor—a small, steady island in the turbulent sea of my professional life. Without prompting, she'd have her notes neatly arranged before I even asked, anticipating needs I hadn't voiced. Between tasks, we shared fleeting moments—once, she offered a sharp, insightful comment on a complex design issue

I'd been wrestling with, a clarity I rarely found in conversations with Neetu.

I began to look forward to those glimpses of her: the curve of her smile when our eyes met across the room, the calm strength in her voice as she navigated demanding clients, and the way she met every challenge I handed her with effortless grace.

She didn't just impress me—she intrigued me.

One evening, after a long meeting with a particularly abrasive client, the tension still knotting my shoulders, I leaned back in my chair, utterly drained. Sonam, as usual, was organizing the paperwork. The soft rustle of documents was a familiar sound as she sorted through the contracts, her back to me. Her calm and composed demeanour was a stark contrast to my own, still reeling from the intensity of the meeting.

"Sonam," I called out, my voice a little more weary than usual.

She turned around, her brow slightly furrowed with concern, her gaze holding its usual calm. "Yes, Mr. Singh?"

I hesitated momentarily, the question forming almost without conscious thought, then asked, "How do you manage to stay so calm under all this pressure?"

She smiled lightly, a subtle crinkle appearing at the corner of her eyes, and sat across from me, folding her arms with an air of quiet composure. "I think it's all about perspective. You learn to see things for what they are. In the end, it's just work."

Her calm demeanour and insightful words were like a soothing balm, reassuring me that there's always a way to maintain composure even in the most challenging situations.

Her words lingered in the air, and I felt a genuine sense of ease in her presence for the first time, a lightness I hadn't realized I was craving. Something about her steady gaze and the unwavering confidence in her voice made the weight of everything else seem less crushing. Her perspective on work was not just a personal mantra but a source of inspiration for me to approach my challenges with a similar calm and understanding.

"That's... a good way to look at it," I said. Then, almost involuntarily, I confessed something I hadn't intended to voice: "I wish I could be as calm as you sometimes."

Sonam let out a soft chuckle, a warm sound that filled the quiet office. Her eyes held mine a moment longer than usual, and the subtle warmth in them made my pulse quicken almost imperceptibly.

"It's all about balance, Mr. Singh," she said. "You just need to find it."

I nodded, though the concept felt abstract and distant. Inside, however, a different question was taking root. Was it truly balance I needed, or something else entirely—a connection, a feeling of being truly seen?

The city lights blurred outside the window as I walked to the elevator after another late night at the office. I found myself wondering about her more than I'd like to admit. There was something magnetic about how she carried herself—confident and composed—yet she exuded a quiet kindness in the supportive words she offered and the knowing glances she shared. It was a kindness I hadn't consciously recognized before.

Suddenly, as if a switch clicked, I returned to the familiar landscape of my life and caught a fleeting, almost obligatory glimpse of Neetu's tired face in my mind. Yet the image of Sonam, with her calm gaze, and soft chuckle, lingered longer, like a persistent echo in the elevator's silence.

I had become so engrossed in the intricate lines of a new design—a welcome distraction from the day's gnawing unease—that I didn't realize how much time had slipped away. When I finally glanced at the clock, the digital numbers glowed ominously at 10 p.m. The office was eerily silent, the usual hum of computers and quiet phone calls completely absent. Neetu was away at her parents' place for the week, leaving the apartment feeling hollow and echoing, so there was no immediate pressure to return to that quiet solitude.

As I switched off the cool fluorescent light in my cabin and stepped into the dim hallway, a soft, rhythmic clacking of keys—persistent yet subdued—caught my attention. A flicker of curiosity and a desire for some human contact before the silence of home drew me toward Sonam's desk. There she was, completely immersed in the soft glow of her screen, her brow furrowed in concentration as she refined architectural plans and meticulously added new layers of research. She didn't notice my presence until I stood right beside her. When our eyes finally met, a momentary surprise widened hers, quickly followed by a faint, almost shy smile. I gently suggested that she wrap up; the lateness of the hour suddenly felt significant. She readily agreed, and soon, the automatic doors hissed shut behind us as we stepped out into the cool, damp night air.

The night air, heavy with the promise of rain, filled my lungs—a refreshing contrast to the recycled office atmosphere. The strong, earthy scent felt grounding, and seemed to lift the edges of weariness clinging to us both. Just as we were about to part ways at the curb, an unspoken understanding passed between us. Sonam turned to me and asked, her voice soft and almost hesitant, "Would you… Would you like to walk by the beach? The rain hasn't truly started yet."

My first thought was, "Under this heavy sky? At this late hour?" But something in her quiet tone, a subtle invitation to step outside our usual roles and routines, made it feel like a chance to breathe, to escape the weight of unspoken pressures. I nodded, a silent agreement passing between us, and we strolled in quiet companionship toward the distant sound of the shore.

The beach was hauntingly beautiful in its deserted state. The only sound was the constant, soothing rhythm of waves meeting the dark sand. The cool breeze kissed my skin with a tenderness I hadn't felt in a long time, as if the air was whispering permission to let go of the tight knot in my chest. I walked a few steps ahead and sank into the cool, yielding sand, the ocean's music pulling me into a stillness I hadn't realized I needed so desperately.

As the gentle patter of rain began, it felt like a cleansing, washing away both the dust and grime of the day and something deeper weighing on my heart. A wave of emotion, unexpected, and overwhelming, washed over me. I smiled and cried at the same time—relieved to finally feel something genuine, anything beyond the dull ache of my everyday life. In that unguarded moment, Sonam quietly sat beside me. The soft rustle of her jacket was the only sound besides the rain and the waves. She didn't say a word; her presence was a silent acknowledgement of my pain. She rested her hand on my shoulder, and the warmth seeped through my damp shirt, serving as a steady, reassuring anchor. It was a moment of emotional release, a catharsis I longed for.

Her touch wasn't possessive or demanding; it was a gentle offering of human connection, a quiet understanding that transcended words. I turned to thank her, a choked sound escaping my lips—more a breath than a coherent word. She responded with a soft, empathetic smile, and gently brushed away the single tear that had traced a path down my cheek, her fingers as light as a feather. An overwhelming urge for comfort and connection surged through me, and as if it were the most natural thing in the world, I reached for her hand and pulled her into a close embrace. In that moment, I felt the transformative power of our connection, a bond that went beyond words and actions.

She leaned into me, resting her head on my shoulder, her hair soft against my cheek. We sat quietly, two figures silhouetted against the dark expanse of the ocean, lost in the rhythmic sound of the waves and something unspoken, something tender and new that we couldn't quite name just yet.

That night, something shifted irreversibly between us. What had begun as a quiet, professional companionship gradually blossomed into a meaningful friendship—a space where we could be ourselves without pretence. We started spending time together after work, sharing quiet laughter over coffee, collaborating on projects with newfound ease, and simply enjoying each other's presence. We were no longer just bosses and secretaries; the rigid lines of hierarchy began to blur. We became a team, and a silent understanding grew between us.

She brought in new clients with her sharp insights and fresh perspectives that invigorated my work. Her presence quietly and patiently gathered the unspoken gaps in my day, the moments of loneliness, and quiet desperation, as if something scattered within me was being made whole.

She didn't demand space in my life; she made room for herself. Her presence felt like a natural fit without any forced trying. In her quiet, unassuming way, she reminded me what it felt like to be truly seen, not just for my professional achievements, but for the vulnerable human being beneath.

Once again, Neetu was armed with her familiar arsenal of complaints, each word a tiny barb directed at me whenever I returned home, the lingering scent of Sonam's perfume on my clothes a silent accusation. I had grown apathetic to Neetu's emotional outbursts, a dull weariness settling over me like a heavy shroud. Our relationship had reached a breaking point—strained and worn out, the threads so frayed they seemed impossible to mend. I had come to accept the strain, the weight of it settling on my shoulders like a burden.

"You don't even try to understand me anymore," she often accused, her voice sharp with resentment, while I sat in heavy silence, the energy for argument long since depleted.

At first, she would wait for me at the dinner table, maintaining a silent vigil filled with expectation. However, that had stopped months ago, replaced by a cold indifference that I could not shake off.

"If you're hungry," she would say, her tone flat and devoid of warmth, "you know where the kitchen is."

Our choices over even the simplest things became battlegrounds. If I preferred quiet, Neetu would immediately respond with loud, emphatic opposition—a deliberate act of defiance. The atmosphere was growing bitter, marked by a constant undercurrent of animosity. Eventually, I stopped trying to elicit any positive response or connection. Without realizing it, my heart, starved for warmth, began to seek solace in the gentle image of Sonam.

In the office, I noticed hushed whispers, and sidelong glances directed at Sonam and me. Strangely, the judgement of others hardly affected me. A part of me almost welcomed the attention as it silently acknowledged a truth I was reluctant to express.

One evening, the tension at home finally reached its breaking point. Neetu insisted, her voice rising, that I visit her family to fulfil a long-standing obligation. I refused; the thought of forced pleasantries felt unbearable.

She snapped, her eyes blazing with anger. "You've changed, Sumeet. You're not the man I married."

The words slipped out cold and detached: "Maybe I got tired of pretending to be."

Her shout echoed in the sterile living room as I yelled back, my voice raw with frustration. At that moment, something fragile inside me finally shattered—a dam holding back a torrent of unspoken unhappiness gave way. I felt a mix of relief and fear, a need to breathe, and escape the suffocating atmosphere. I stepped out into the night without a destination in mind and instinctively fumbled for my phone, Sonam's number being the first that came to mind.

My voice was low and thick with unshed tears, as if I were almost on the verge of defeat. "Sonam… I—I just needed to talk."

She didn't question my distress. Her tone was calm, soothing, inviting, and free of judgement. "Come over. You don't have to say a word. Just come."

It was my first time visiting her apartment. As the elevator doors slid open on the fifth floor, she stood just outside her doorway, a soft light spilling from within. Her presence felt like a beacon amidst my turmoil, a quiet homecoming. The warm, inviting atmosphere of her home was a stark contrast to the sterile tension of my own. My eyes welled up, and a lump formed in my throat, overwhelmed by the genuine warmth in her gentle expression. I couldn't remember the last time someone had waited for me like that, without expectation, or recrimination.

She gently took my hand, her touch surprisingly strong and steady, and said softly, "Let's go inside, You look utterly exhausted."

She served dinner—a simple lentil stew, warm naan, and a side of cooling yoghurt—each offering quiet comfort. As she placed a steaming bowl before me, she gently said, "You don't need to speak tonight. Just be."

Later, while we stood on the small balcony, the glittering tapestry of city lights spread behind her like a silent witness. She asked gently, her gaze searching mine, “Did today hurt more than usual?”

I nodded. The simple question unlocked a fresh wave of emotion, and I managed a choked whisper, “I feel… lost.”

Without hesitation, she reached out, and pulled me into a comforting hug, resting her head on my chest, her hair soft against my cheek. “You don’t have to be strong all the time, Sumeet,” she murmured, her voice a soothing vibration against my shirt.

That was the first time she called me by my name, Sumeet, instead of the formal “Mr. Singh.” Its intimacy resonated deeply within me. It meant something; it was a quiet acknowledgement of a shift in our connection.

I held her closer, the scent of her shampoo a comforting familiarity.

“I love you, Sonam,” I whispered, the words escaping before I could fully process them. I was unsure if it was the right time, but I was sure it was the raw, unfiltered truth.

She smiled through misty eyes, a gentle sadness lingering in their depths. “I’ve never really known love in the way you mean it, Sumeet. But I do know this—being with you makes me believe it’s possible. Maybe some of us aren’t meant to chase our grand dreams. Perhaps we’re here to help others find theirs.”

I looked at her, feeling a mixture of curiosity and concern. Was that really how she viewed herself—someone who made others happy instead of seeking her happiness? It surprised me that someone as lovely, warm, and inherently thoughtful as Sonam carried such quiet shadows within her perspective. That night, for the first time, she cautiously opened up about her past, allowing me to glimpse inside.

She spoke of a past filled with disappointment and the

oppressive weight of expectation. Her voice remained calm, but her words conveyed a deep, unspoken pain. “I had dreams, you know,” she said quietly, her gaze distant. “I wanted to work in a field I was passionate about, travel the world, and build something meaningful for myself. But my father was too strict and controlling. Even after I got married, hoping for some freedom, nothing changed. My husband and his family only wanted a traditional housewife—someone to take care of their needs.”

I listened without interrupting, the injustice of her situation settling like a weight in my chest. It was hard to reconcile the composed, vibrant Sonam I knew with the image of a woman who felt held back.

“We were only a year into our marriage when I got pregnant,” she continued, her gaze drifting out into the night sky. “But I had a miscarriage. My health wasn’t strong, and after that, he changed. The small affection that had been there withered. He became distant and cold, as if blaming me for the loss.”

Unshed tears glistened in her eyes, which she quickly blinked away.

“We fought a lot. I tried to hold on, to be everything they wanted—a good wife, a dutiful daughter-in-law—but I couldn’t breathe anymore; the expectations were suffocating me. After two and a half years, I walked away, leaving behind everything that was supposed to be my life.”

She paused for a moment, her voice trembling faintly. “No one stood by me—not even my parents, who saw it as a personal failure. I fought that battle entirely alone. And one day, I won. I got the divorce and came to India from Canada to start over, to build a life on my terms.” Her courage in making this decision was truly inspiring.

My chest ached with profound empathy for her, and I

instinctively wanted to reach out and offer comfort. Instead, I spoke gently, choosing my words carefully. "You're courageous, Sonam. Not everyone has the strength to choose peace and their well-being over the perceived security of familiarity."

She gave a faint, almost weary smile. "I'm just tired of being told who I should be, Sumeet."

Then she mentioned how she got the job through a friend who had recommended Dr. Kapoor—a name that sparked a small, knowing smile on my face.

"He's one of the best," I said, warmth filling my voice.

"He helped me through a lot, too." This shared connection between us brought a sense of unity and understanding.

Her eyes softened at that shared connection.

"Life's about taking chances," I added, meeting her eyes.

"You can't let the pain of the past dictate the story of your future. And no matter what, you should never be afraid to fall in love again, Sonam."

She tilted her head, her expression thoughtful, as if carefully considering my words, but offered no immediate reply. The weight of the past gradually lifted as our conversation shifted, meandering through lighter topics. The air grew lighter as we shared quiet laughter and stories from our childhoods—funny work anecdotes and the strange, unexpected quirks of life.

Later, as the evening deepened, she leaned back into the soft cushions of the sofa, stretching her neck with a slight wince of discomfort.

"Ouch… this neck pain won't let me breathe," she murmured, her eyes closing slightly in discomfort.

"Do you want me to help?" I had an instinctive desire to ease her pain rising within me.

She raised a playful eyebrow, a hint of her earlier lightness returning. "Are you a doctor now, too, Sumeet?"

I grinned, a genuine smile spreading across my face. "I'm told I have healing hands. In another life, I might have been a masseur."

She giggled, the sound bright, and melodic in the quiet apartment. "My feet are next, then…"

We both laughed, the shared moment easing the earlier intensity. I moved closer and gently touched Sonam's shoulders, feeling the taut muscles beneath my fingertips. As I pressed into the knots and tension, I felt her body gradually relax beneath my touch, a subtle sigh escaping her lips. My touch was a source of warmth and reassurance for her.

"You're not joking," she whispered, her eyes still closed in contentment.

"I told you," I said softly, my voice low, and intimate.

Her pain seemed to melt away under my touch as I worked in comfortable silence, my fingers tracing along the delicate curves of her shoulders and neck. The closeness felt natural and comforting, not rushed, or demanding. She didn't move away, and for that brief, suspended moment, we both seemed to forget the weight of the past and the complexities of the present.

Her skin, a stark contrast to the rough demands of my architectural drawings, held the lingering warmth of a summer evening. It was as smooth as the finest silk, a texture I had never experienced professionally. The scent of her hair, a delicate blend I couldn't quite identify, evoked the image of a hidden garden after a refreshing rain shower, drawing me closer with an irresistible pull.

A silent question hung between us, forming a fragile bridge of unspoken desire. I lowered my lips to her neck, delivering the slightest whisper of a kiss against Sonam's pulse point. She smiled softly, with a knowing curve of her lips that hinted at a shared understanding deeper than words could express. At that moment, the familiar weight of my responsibilities, the guilt, and the world outside her embrace vanished completely.

What was it about Sonam's quiet strength and unwavering empathy that made me abandon all the carefully constructed rules I had lived by and the boundaries I had erected around my heart? Her influence was so profound that it led me to question the very foundations of my life.

Cupping her face in my hands, I gently traced the delicate curve of her cheekbones with my thumbs. I lowered my lips to hers, the touch tentative at first, a gentle exploration that deepened with a sudden, undeniable urgency. It felt like I was finally filling a long space within her—a void I hadn't fully understood until now. Her soft sigh in response—a breathy surrender—resonated deep within my soul like a melody I hadn't known I was missing. Her hands found my waist in a silent, anchoring embrace that spoke volumes of our trust and the love blossoming between us.

"You've awakened something in me," she whispered, her breath warm, and slightly unsteady against my lips—a vulnerability I had never witnessed before. I lowered my head, my lips brushing the delicate shell of her ear, the faint scent of her skin intoxicating.

"And you have awakened in me a longing I never knew I possessed, a yearning for a connection that transcends the surface of my days."

There was no more hesitation, no more holding back. My kisses traced the delicate curve of Sonam's neck, each a silent promise, as our bodies instinctively drew closer, seeking the comfort of skin against skin. My fingers trembled with anticipation and tenderness as I undid the buttons, the soft rustle of fabric providing a quiet backdrop to our quickening breaths. The heat between us was undeniable, a palpable energy wrapped in a profound softness and mutual care, a gentleness that communicated so much. Every caress, every shared sigh, deepened the invisible bond that had begun forming long before this night in the quiet moments we spent together.

Sonam's breath quickened, a soft gasp escaping her lips as she held me close, her body arching slightly in silent surrender to the moment. We moved with a slow, deliberate rhythm, like a dance we instinctively knew, each step guided by an unspoken understanding. Her warmth enveloped me in a comforting embrace, and her quiet joy spilt forth in delicate murmurs against my skin. Her touch ignited a fire across my senses, a gentle conflagration.

There was no need for the clumsy inadequacy of words. Our bodies spoke a language we both understood, and every shared moment felt sacred, like rediscovering a vital part of ourselves that we had long forgotten, a sense of being truly alive and connected.

As the first light of dawn filtered through the curtains, casting soft shadows across the room, we lay together, wrapped in the comfortable silence of each other's arms. We interlaced our hands, a tangible symbol of our intertwined emotions. We whispered about the complexities of love, the unexpected turns of life, about everything, and yet somehow nothing. It was the comfortable ease of shared intimacy. I didn't want the fragile beauty of the night to end; the newfound peace I had found in her arms felt too precious to let go.

I woke early, the same soft light of dawn now painting the room in gentle hues. Watching Sonam sleep peacefully, her dark hair spread across the white pillow like a spilt ink poem, I felt an overwhelming warmth. A selfish part of me, filled with a desperate yearning for this newfound tranquillity, wanted to pause time, and etch this warmth into eternity. Yet, even in that blissful embrace, a cold knot of reality tightened in my stomach;

I knew the luminous illusion of that stolen night would soon blur with the muted grey of the life I had consciously left behind—the weight of my choices, guilt, and longing mingled in a tumultuous storm within me. I was beginning to understand the price of my happiness.

From that day on, Sonam, and I became inseparable—two lovebirds navigating a clandestine world of stolen moments. Each touch and each whispered word became a precious rebellion against my stagnant existence. She brought a vibrant spectrum of colour to a life I hadn't realized had faded into a monochrome of routine and obligation. As my marriage to Neetu grew increasingly distant and hollow, marked by strained silences, and unspoken resentments, my weekends transformed into carefully orchestrated escapes—to her sun-drenched apartment, to quiet resorts hidden from prying eyes, to those fleeting moments when only Sonam and I existed. It was a world built on whispered promises and shared secrets. Yet, I couldn't shake the guilt I felt towards Neetu, the woman I had once loved and who had stood by me through thick and thin.

With Sonam, I rediscovered a love that felt effortless and genuine. She asked for nothing beyond my presence and affection. She never complained about our secretive time together or our constant need for discretion. She loved me with a pure and unwavering devotion that was a balm to my weary soul.

That morning, the ordinary showering was interrupted by the familiar chime of my phone. Sonam's usual early message of love flashed across the screen, serving as a sweet, and simple reminder of the vibrant beauty we had found together. *"Thinking of you,"* it read, accompanied by a small heart emoji. However, the casual intimacy of that digital affection was a ticking time bomb that I hadn't noticed. I didn't realize Neetu, whose sleep had been disturbed by my early rising, was near my phone.

When I walked back into the bedroom, the steam from the shower still clinging to my skin, I felt an immediate shift in the atmosphere—an unsettling tension hung heavily in the air. There were no tears, raised voices, or familiar accusations—just a chilling, unnerving silence. Neetu sat rigidly on the edge of the bed, her back to me, her posture radiating a stillness that unsettled me more profoundly than any of her previous emotional outbursts.

It wasn't until later that I noticed the faint tremor in her hand as she held her teacup and the unnatural brightness in her averted gaze.

At the office, a knot of anxiety tightened in my chest. I longed for the familiar comfort of normalcy, but Sonam's desk was starkly empty. She was the embodiment of punctuality, never late—not even by a precise minute. A quiet, icy panic spread through me, chilling my usual focus. I called her number, my finger hovering over the screen. Each unanswered ring amplified my unease once, twice, and then again.

In the late afternoon, just as the last rays of sunlight slanted through my window, the door to my cabin creaked open with a hesitant groan. Sonam stepped in slowly, her usual vibrant energy completely extinguished. Her face was pale as parchment, and her eyes held a distant, unfocused quality. A wave of relief, so potent it almost buckled my knees, washed over me at the sight of her. However, the subtle tremor in her hands and the hollowness in her gaze told me this was far from another ordinary day.

She reached into her worn leather bag, moving slowly and deliberately, and handed me a crisp white envelope. My fingers felt clumsy as I opened it, a sense of foreboding settling in. The stark finality of what I held in my trembling hands—a neatly typed resignation letter—caught me unprepared.

I looked up at her in disbelief, fighting rising terror. "Sonam… what is this? Is everything alright?"

Her lips trembled, a delicate flutter like a trapped bird before any words could escape. Heavy with unspoken sorrow, silent tears began to spill down her pale cheeks, leaving glistening tracks.

I moved closer, an instinctive need to comfort her overriding my growing fear. I gently placed a hand on her cool shoulder. "Talk to me… please."

She nodded, a slight, jerky movement as she fought to compose herself. In a soft voice, each word catching in her throat, she spoke, broken yet achingly honest.

"This morning… before I left home, my phone rang. It was Neetu."

A cold stillness, heavier than any physical weight, settled over me as if the air had solidified, pausing the relentless march of time.

"She saw our messages... and the chats. She knows everything now, Sumeet. Everything we shared. Her voice was so cold when she told me to walk away from your life. For good."

I felt as though I had turned to stone, my limbs heavy and unresponsive, unable to offer comfort, or even speak past the sudden constriction in my chest.

"There were arguments," Sonam continued, her voice barely above a whisper, "but your wife… she was resolute. She made it clear—she isn't giving up on you, Sumeet. She wants me to be the one who steps away, to erase myself from your world."

I took a deep, shuddering breath, the air feeling thin, and insufficient, yet my mind was surprisingly clear amidst the swirling chaos of my emotions.

"And what do you want, Sonam?" I asked, my voice low, and urgent.

She didn't answer. She fixed her gaze on a point beyond me, her eyes heavy with a profound pain that mirrored my own—a pain I couldn't bear to witness.

I took her hands in mine, my grip firm, hoping to offer strength.

"Listen to me, Sonam. I am not letting you go. Not out of guilt for what's happened, and not out of fear of being alone. I chose you that night on the beach, in every stolen moment since—and I still choose you, unequivocally. I'm willing to walk away from my marriage and the life I thought I wanted. But I won't, I can't walk away from us."

She looked at me, her expression a fragile tapestry woven with love, fear, and heartbreaking selflessness.

"I never wanted to break anyone's home, Sumeet," she whispered, her voice thick with unshed tears.

"I know," I said, my thumbs gently stroking the back of her hands.

"But love doesn't always come neatly wrapped. Sometimes, it finds us in the wreckage, after we've already lost pieces of ourselves. And when it does—when it's this real—we have to hold on, Sonam. We have to fight for it."

Sonam didn't respond immediately, her gaze searching mine as a silent battle raged within her. The tears silently streaming down her face began to ease, leaving her eyes glistening. She gave me a look—half raw love, half fragile hope—and finally, a small, hesitant smile touched her lips.

"I'm scared, Sumeet... but... I trust you."

"That's all I ask," I whispered, my voice thick with emotion as I gently brushed a stray tear from her cheek.

"This isn't the end, Sonam. It's the beginning of everything real—everything we've ever truly wanted."

She left my office that day with a fragile, uncertain smile, her unopened resignation letter lying like a silent testament on my otherwise cluttered desk. I stood still amidst the quiet chaos of my cabin, the weight of the impending storm pressing down on me. Yet, a fragile sense of liberation bloomed within my chest for the first time in a long while. I knew the price would be high, but the possibility of a future with Sonam felt worth fighting for.

The late afternoon sun, usually a comforting presence filtering through the office blinds, felt more like a harsh interrogation lamp as it ruthlessly illuminated Neetu by the window. The light highlighted the delicate curve of her growing belly beneath her loose dress. She sat in a stillness that spoke of unspoken burdens, her shoulders slightly slumped, her eyes fixed on the distant, hazy horizon beyond our familiar walls.

I approached her, each step feeling heavy, weighed down by the burden of a confession that threatened to shatter the fragile tapestry of our lives. I sat beside her on the sofa's edge, the silence stretching taut between us, unsure how to begin. My heart felt like a leaden weight carrying a truth that could irrevocably break everything we had built, however flawed.

Before the first syllable could escape my lips, she turned to me. Her eyes shone not with the suspicion I had braced for nor the pain I knew I deserved but with a soft, almost luminous quality—something else entirely, a gentle happiness.

"I'm pregnant," she whispered, her voice barely audible. Yet each syllable resonated in the quiet room like the solemn tolling of bells. Time seemed to stutter, momentarily pausing its relentless march. My breath caught in my throat, a sudden, sharp intake. For a fleeting instant, my mind went utterly blank.

Two and a half months along. After eight long years of navigating a landscape filled with unspoken disappointments and growing distance, we were finally expecting a child.

That single, unexpected moment changed the entire trajectory of my carefully constructed plans, momentarily lifting the weight of my guilt. All the internal chaos—the gnawing guilt, the agonizing decisions I had made, and the profound sorrow of what I was about to lose—faded for a few blissful, disoriented seconds. A choked laugh escaped my lips, devoid of genuine mirth. Tears, a confusing mix of shock and something akin to relief, welled in my eyes. Suddenly seized by an impulsive energy, I stood up, and danced a clumsy, foolish jig. I pulled Neetu into my arms; her body was surprisingly pliant, and I kissed her forehead, the soft curve of her cheek, and finally, hesitantly, her lips.

For the first time in what felt like forever, I felt her arms around me, not out of habit, or obligation, but with a tenderness that radiated genuine, forgiving love. It was a sensation I hadn't known in years—a forgotten sweetness. A fragile peace settled over me, which should have warmed me from the inside out. Instead, it shattered me from within. The weight of my deception became suddenly unbearable. In that moment of unexpected grace, I knew, with chilling certainty, that everything had changed.

I knew I was living a lie, accepting a love I no longer deserved. Feelings are like wild winds—unpredictable, intense, and fleeting. One moment, you're soaring on the updraft of joy, and the next, you're plummeting into the suffocating silence of regret.

That night, I lay beside Neetu as she slept soundly, her hand resting protectively on the slight swell of her belly. The rhythmic rise and fall of her breathing stood in stark contrast to the turmoil within me. I stared at the unyielding expanse of the ceiling, drowning in a torrent of thoughts that offered no moment of respite.

My worn leather office bag sat innocently by the door, a silent sentinel guarding my fractured reality. Inside, nestled among my papers, were two stark envelopes.

One moment held the crisp divorce papers I had signed earlier that day—a decisive act meant to sever my ties with Neetu and finally leave the hollow shell of our marriage behind. The other moment contained Sonam's carefully typed resignation letter, which was still unsigned, and a testament to my wavering resolve.

But after Neetu's unexpected news, my determination crumbled. I froze, caught between two impossible choices. I couldn't give her those papers now; I couldn't shatter her newfound joy or take away the father of her child before that child had even taken its first breath.

So, I stayed quiet, a hollow echo in the stillness of our bedroom. I closed my eyes, feigning sleep, but the relentless churn of my thoughts kept me tethered to the agonizing present.

At dawn, my fingers trembled with fear and a desperate need for resolution as I composed a short message to Sonam: "Please come see me at the office."

The sterile environment of my cabin—once a haven for focused creativity—offered no solace today. Instead, it echoed with the chaos storming inside me. The chill that clung to my hands mirrored the numbness tightening around my heart. On the polished surface of my desk lay two stark white sheets—unforgiving in their simplicity, each one a silent witness to the lives I had irreversibly changed.

These two papers stood before me as silent judgements. Two paths diverged, both shrouded in pain, and both would inevitably break someone I cared for deeply.

Regardless of the choice I made, I knew with sickening certainty that I would lose an essential piece of myself.

If I chose Sonam, I would be deliberately taking a father

away from my unborn child, condemning that innocent life to a fractured beginning. I would be tearing apart a woman who, despite everything, still believed in the possibility of second chances and held a fragile hope for our future. But if I chose Neetu, I would betray the only woman who had truly touched the deepest corners of my soul and showed me what it felt like to be seen and loved unconditionally.

My circumstances had changed irrevocably, but the stubborn truth of my heart remained the same. Affairs may come and go like fleeting shadows, leaving only faint traces behind; however, some love stories, no matter how brief, leave permanent, indelible marks.

Some decisions, no matter how logically right they may seem, still leave you bleeding internally, with wounds that are unseen but agonisingly real. I sat hunched over in my cabin, the weak morning sun spilling across my desk and illuminating the two envelopes before me like stark instruments of fate, waiting for my hand to seal their destinies.

One envelope contained the fragile promise of a future, however fraught, with Neetu, and our unborn child. The other held a final, silent goodbye to the woman who had awakened my soul. Both demanded my signature—a simple act with devastating consequences—and came at an unbearable cost.

I stared at them, my hand hovering inches above the stark white paper, paralyzed by the weight of my decision.

My heart beat frantically against my ribs, a desperate drumbeat echoing in the silence. I breathed in shallow, uneven gasps.

Because I knew with chilling certainty—whichever option I chose, whichever path I signed… My signature would irrevocably break someone. Neetu's and Sonam's shattering would hurt me, too.

When Sonam finally arrived, her presence was a fragile question mark in the doorway; I couldn't bring myself to meet her gaze. I didn't feel worthy of the unwavering love reflected in her searching eyes.

She walked in quietly, her usual composed demeanour replaced by raw vulnerability. Her eyes scanned my face and the room, desperately looking for answers I didn't dare to provide—words that remained trapped in my throat.

Slowly and deliberately, she picked up the two envelopes from my desk, her fingers tracing their crisp edges. She opened them one by one, her movements betraying a tremor she tried to conceal.

Her eyes scanned the familiar words of her resignation; her name typed neatly at the top. My signature, a stark black mark against the white, confirmed her fears.

The second envelope—the divorce papers—remained stubbornly unsigned, a silent testament to my agonizing indecision.

She didn't say a single word, look at me, or ask the question that lingered like smoke between us: 'Why?'

Instead, with a quiet grace that belied the storm within her, she folded the two papers back, her movements precise and controlled, and stepped closer to my desk.

She gently pulled out a carefully wrapped object from her small purse—a green silk tie, the shade she had admired on me just days before, the one she had thoughtfully chosen for my birthday today. She remembered. Even amidst the devastating unravelling… she remembered.

Neetu had not acknowledged the day at all—not a single word of greeting, not even a passing glance. But Sonam had still brought me a gift, a small, tangible piece of love wrapped in quiet dignity.

Her hands trembled almost imperceptibly as she reached

up to my collar, her touch feather-light. One last time, with exquisite care, she tied the tie for me, her fingers pausing at the knot, holding on for a fraction of a second longer—as if trying to preserve one final, tactile memory of our connection.

Her tears fell silently, tracing glistening paths down her pale cheeks like soft, sorrowful rain. Finally, looking straight into my eyes, her gaze unwavering despite the immense pain I knew I was inflicting—her voice surprisingly steady, her heart visibly breaking—she whispered, the simple words carrying the weight of a thousand unspoken goodbyes: "Happy Birthday, Sumeet."

The simple, heartfelt wish, offered amidst such profound sorrow, struck me like a physical blow—a kindness I knew I didn't deserve. It was a final, selfless act of love that tore through my carefully constructed defences, shattering the last remnants of my composure.

That one small wish, given with such grace and heartbreak, broke me more completely than any tearful accusation or bitter goodbye ever could.

She stepped back, a faint, heartbreakingly fragile smile gracing her lips —a ghost of the joy they had once shared.

"I'm not going to ask you for any explanation, Sumeet," she said, her voice soft yet imbued with quiet strength.

Then, with a quiet dignity that left me utterly hollowed out, she turned, and walked away. Her departure was absolute, final. There was no backwards glance, no lingering hint of hope in her retreating figure. She didn't need to look back. In the depths of her knowing heart, she already understood.

Sonam returned to her silent world, carrying the immense weight of her broken heart like a precious, fragile thing—a treasure she would guard in its shattered state. She would likely never fully comprehend the complex forces that had driven my agonizing decision or the brutal internal battle that had torn me apart, leaving me a fractured version of the man she loved. She would never truly know the enduring depth of my love for her, a love now buried beneath suffocating layers of guilt and a crushing sense of responsibility.

Neetu would always be the mother of my child, and I would dedicate myself to that child with every fibre of my being, pouring all my efforts into being the father they deserved.

But Sonam… she would forever remain the woman who held the key to the deepest corners of my soul, the one whose love had illuminated the darkest recesses of my heart. Unfortunately, my actions had now extinguished that light.

Today, I shattered her heart into a million irreparable pieces. Yet, she would never know the full extent of the collateral damage—the countless fragments of myself that broke alongside hers, leaving me a hollow shell forever haunted by the ghost of what could have been.

Swapped

To the outside world, we seemed like just another happily married couple. But to each other, we were everything.

My name is Sunny, and even after all these years, Nisha—my wife and my forever—still has the power to pause my world with just her smile, even after twelve years of marriage. The way her eyes crinkle at the corners is a familiar kind of magic that never fades. Our bond isn't just a marriage, but a profound connection that transcends time and space.

Our story began like a fairytale, with a wedding on the sun-kissed shores of the Maldives, where the ocean witnessed our vows and the breeze whispered promises we still strive to keep. I remember the salty air and the warmth of her hand, steady in mine. Our journey from India to California was not just a relocation but a shared adventure that saw our careers flourishing in the dynamic heart of a leading financial travel firm. The years blessed us with friendships that deepened into kinship and laughter; the aroma of shared meals and intimate conversations filled our home on weekends, conveying an unspoken understanding between our souls.

Sometimes, while watching her across a crowded room, I would feel a fresh wave of gratitude for the life we've built. Our connection ran deeper than mere companionship. Even after years of marriage, the spark between us never dwindled. We embraced our desires and were bold in our intimacy. Every corner of our home held a memory, a whisper of closeness. I would tease her with cheeky jokes to see the delicate blush creeping up her neck, blooming into a beautiful, bashful pink. She would roll her eyes, a small smile on her lips, and I would fall in love with her all over again, a love that remains as strong and vibrant as it was on our wedding day.

But then, something shifted.

Earlier today, what started as a playful conversation with Nisha about a silly work anecdote took a turn. An uneasy tension crept in—not dramatic, but a subtle tightening in my chest as her smile faltered for a fleeting moment. We began with light-hearted banter, but at some point, my thoughts became tangled, and the easy rhythm of our conversation was abruptly interrupted by a hesitation in her voice. For someone who is usually so self-assured, I fumbled for words, feeling a strange disorientation settle over me. The rest of the day passed in a fog, and the usual hum of our home felt muted. That one moment, that almost imperceptible shift in the air, clung to me—silent and stubborn, like a tiny seed of doubt taking root. It always returns every Christmas, like clockwork. As lights twinkle and carols play, a specific image flickers in my mind: the muted silver of a forgotten ornament, casting a subtle shadow over the forced joy of the season. It's a feeling I can't quite shake, a persistent whisper of something... amiss.

A few years later…

It was December again, and everyone was running on empty. Work was piling up as we raced to close the year. Even after leaving the office, we remained glued to our laptops, our minds buzzing with emails and deadlines. Time felt scarce, and the pressure weighed heavily on us, a constant hum beneath the surface of our days. The festive spirit was present—twinkling in shop windows and playing softly on the radio—but it hadn't arrived for us yet.

Finally, after weeks of nonstop work, we were gifted a rare break—an escape we both desperately needed. The timing couldn't have been better; it felt like a lifeline thrown amidst the year-end storm. One of our dear friends had invited us to spend the weekend at their countryside farm, and the thought of it was like a breath of fresh, cool air waiting to embrace us.

Eager for a change of pace, we gathered a few close friends and set off for a getaway. The drive felt therapeutic, with rolling hills unfolding like green velvet carpets, golden fields stretching toward the horizon, and winding roads lined with trees still adorned in the rich hues of late autumn.

When we arrived, our warm-hearted hosts, Jacky and Lee, were already waiting at the gate. Their faces lit up with the welcome that instantly made you feel at ease, as if returning to a place you truly belonged.

"There they are!" Jacky called out, waving both hands above his head, his enthusiasm infectious.

"About time!" Lee teased, laughing as she rushed forward to hug Nisha. Her embrace was warm and genuine.

"We were beginning to think you got lost in the vineyards."

"Well, blame Sunny. He stopped every few minutes to take pictures." Nisha grinned, pulling away from the hug, a playful glint in her eyes. "I think we have half of California's countryside saved on our phones now."

"Guilty," I said with a shrug, a smile tugging at my lips. "But can you blame me? This place is stunning."

Their hugs were tight and heartfelt, wrapping around you like a warm blanket. Jacky and Lee, both Americans deeply in love, had been living together for a while, their easy affection a constant presence. With their wedding just around the corner, it was our first visit to their farm.

The following morning, Jacky invited us to explore the garden that the previous owner had recently acquired. Jacky held a vibrant dream for what was once a barren patch of land.

"Come on, I want you to see the new garden area," Jacky said after breakfast, his voice bubbling with excitement and lifting the morning air. "It's still a work in progress, but I have big plans for it."

"I can't wait," Nisha said, smiling as she slipped her hand into mine, her touch a familiar comfort. "Jacky's ideas always turn out magical."

As we wandered through the vast grounds, a soft breeze carried the earthy scent of turned soil and the delicate fragrance of blooming flowers. Tall fruit trees stood heavy with vibrant colours—sun-drenched oranges glowing like jewels, ripe mangoes hanging low, and sweet berries bursting. Exotic birds called from a distance, their melodies weaving through the peaceful atmosphere, while curious animals roamed freely, adding to the farm's gentle charm.

"Did you see that?" Lee pointed toward a white peacock strutting gracefully near the fence, its iridescent tail feathers shimmering in the sunlight.

"I thought those only existed in fairytales," I said, pulling out my phone as my photographer's instinct kicked in.

"No pictures yet," Jacky grinned, playfully shaking his head. "Wait till you see the heart of the garden."

Entering the garden felt like stepping into a secret world, a hushed sanctuary. Tall stone walls embraced the space, covered in flowering vines that danced with every whisper of the wind, their blossoms a riot of colour. Stone paths curled gracefully through the lush greenery, guiding us deeper into the garden toward the centre—a circular flower bed within a square of perfectly manicured grass, a vibrant splash of life against the green.

Jacky's eyes sparkled as he began explaining his vision. "I want this to be our little sanctuary," he said, his voice softening with affection.

"Picture us enjoying evenings with wine, feet in the grass, while Lee reads some classic novel out loud and I grill something on the patio…"

Lee laughed, her sound warm, and melodic. "You romantic fool. You want an excuse to plant twenty more types of roses."

"And you just want an excuse to read 'Wuthering Heights' in every corner of the house," Jacky countered, his eyes twinkling.

We all chuckled, our shared laughter becoming a light-hearted melody in the tranquil garden.

"Honestly," I added, looking around and feeling a sense of peace settle over me, "this place already feels sacred. You two have created something beautiful here."

Jacky smiled, then paused thoughtfully, a flicker of something deeper reflecting in his eyes. "Thanks, man. I want to make it ours, you know? A space that feels like love."

At that moment, surrounded by vibrant vines, the easy rhythm of our laughter, and the gentle rustling of leaves in nearby trees, I believed he had already succeeded.

Our remaining days at the farm blended seamlessly into shared laughter and easy camaraderie, a balm for our weary souls. As our departure drew near, a quiet understanding settled among us: we would savour our final night, an unspoken agreement to hold on to these precious moments. Gradually, the larger group dispersed, drawn by comfortable armchairs, and quiet conversations, leaving the four of us bathed in the soft, golden glow of the evening.

Soon, the sounds of clinking glasses and the rich aroma of aged spirits filled the air as we settled onto the porch. Conversation flowed as freely as the drinks, fuelled by shared memories, and the relaxed atmosphere. Under the vast, starlit sky, a sense of warmth, and deep connection enveloped us.

"Last night calls for one thing," Jacky announced, lifting two bottles with a cheeky grin, his eyes sparkling with mischief. "Liquid memories."

"Bring it on," Nisha laughed, leaning back in her chair, her earlier weariness forgotten. "But only if we get some music too!"

"Already on it," Lee said, pulling out her phone, and connecting it to the speakers. A smooth, upbeat rhythm filled the air, gently inviting us to unwind.

We poured ourselves generous drinks and raised a toast, the clinking of glasses marking a cheerful pause in the evening.

"To good friends and beautiful endings," I said, raising my glass towards them.

"And maybe new beginnings," Lee added with a knowing wink, her gaze briefly meeting mine.

As the drinks took effect, our inhibitions melted away like morning mist. We placed our glasses down and let the music take over, surrendering to the rhythm. There were no rules or steps to follow—just wild, unfiltered joy expressed in clumsy movements and unrestrained laughter. We danced as if no one were watching, revelling in the carefree spirit of the night.

After hours of joyous abandon, I twirled Nisha one last time, her laughter echoing in the night air. She leaned against me, breathless, her warmth radiating off of me.

"I'm wiped out," she whispered, her voice soft with exhaustion. "I'm heading to bed, love."

I kissed her forehead, a gesture of affection I was familiar with. "Go ahead, baby. I'll hang back a little longer."

Jacky was already on his third drink and riding high, his movements becoming more exaggerated.

"Jacky, slow down a bit," Lee said gently, her concern evident in her voice. "You're going to knock yourself out."

He waved her off with a wide grin. "Let me live, Lee. It's our last night!"

But sure enough, a few minutes later, the alcohol hit him hard. He slurred his words slightly and laughed as he eventually stood up, swaying a bit.

"Alright, I'm tapping out," he announced, his speech a little fuzzy. "The bed is calling my name with a siren song."

And then it was just Lee and me, the remnants of the lively evening settling around us.

We remained seated under the vast expanse of the open sky, the air still warm from shared laughter and the gentle buzz of our drinks. A quiet, unexpected comfort settled between us, enveloped in an unspoken connection.

"Funny, isn't it?" Lee said, tilting her head back to look at the star-dusted canvas above. "You can know people for years and still discover something new in just one night."

I glanced at her, curiosity piqued by her tone. "Like what?"

She smiled, her eyes reflecting a distant, almost dreamy quality illuminated by the starlight. "It's like how poetry sounds better after you've had two glasses of red wine and the moon is putting on a show, painting the world in silver."

"Then hit me with one," I replied, a smile mirroring hers.

She didn't hesitate. Her voice softened, taking on a lyrical quality as she whispered into the quiet night:
"Under Scorpio skies,
Two strangers become a story
Written in moonlight."

There was a pause—not awkward or forced, but filled with a

shared awareness, something unspoken hanging in the starlit air between us.

In that silence, I began to perceive her in a different light. "You always had a way with words," I murmured, the compliment feeling genuine, almost like a revelation.

"Zodiac girl," she chuckled softly, her gaze returning from the stars. "Born under Pisces—what do you expect? An emotional mess with a poetic twist."

I laughed softly with her, gently breaking the stillness around us. The moment stretched—golden and warm—suspended from the usual flow of time. Her perfume lingered in the crisp night air, and somewhere in the distance, the low hum of a passing car threaded reality back into our little bubble.

Then she said quietly, her voice losing its playful tone, a hint of something deeper creeping in.

"Sunny… don't you sometimes wonder if fate swaps timelines? Like, what if we had met differently…?"

I turned fully toward her, trying to decipher the expression in her eyes under the dim starlight. A sudden alertness sharpened my senses.

"Sometimes," I admitted, the word feeling heavier than intended. In that moment, we both seemed lost in our thoughts, a shared moment of introspection.

"But I try not to think too much about the what-ifs. It's a dangerous path."

Our eyes lingered for a moment too long, a silent current passing between us, a flicker of something that felt both familiar and entirely new. Just like that, the comfortable ease of the evening fractured, and something shifted again; the air became charged with an unspoken question. I could feel my heart beating faster, a nervous energy crackling between us.

During our conversation, Lee mentioned a book called *"Stars In You And Me,"* her eyes lighting up with genuine excitement as she described how its zodiac-themed poetry had reawakened a quiet corner of her soul—her love for the written word. She fondly spoke of it, painting pictures of the ethereal verses that lingered in her memory. "It's in our room," Lee said softly, referring to the space she shared with Jacky. I found myself captivated, not just by the imagery she recalled, but by her sheer enthusiasm and the way her voice softened with each carefully chosen word. Though poetry had never called to the pragmatic side of me before, the way Lee's face glowed with wistful beauty stirred something quietly curious within me. Maybe someday I'd ask to borrow it—to see the world through her eyes for a moment.

We sat comfortably on the porch swing, the gentle creaking of the swing matching the rhythmic chirping of crickets. Our drinks were cool in our hands as we let the peaceful sounds of the countryside wrap around us like a comforting blanket. Sharing stories about our star signs started as a lighthearted game, but it soon led us down unexpected paths of personal revelation. We began to uncover the hidden contours of our lives and personalities, revealing vulnerabilities we usually kept guarded. Laughter echoed softly in the stillness as we revisited our teenage dreams, marvelling with fondness at the endearing naiveté of our past selves and the uncomplicated passions of youth. The easy silence shifted, and the comfortable rhythm was interrupted by a subtle change in Lee's posture. She turned toward me, her earlier lightness replaced by a profound earnestness that settled deep in her warm brown gaze. The directness of her look made my heart skip a beat.

"Have you ever thought about just... starting over?" she asked softly, her voice barely above a whisper, carried gently by the night breeze. "A quiet life on this farm. Dogs, maybe kids. Just peace. Just us."

She painted a vivid picture with her words, creating a tapestry of shared dawns that coloured the sky in shades of rose and gold. I could almost hear children's laughter echoing through the fields, mingling with the joyful barks of dogs. It was a life lived deeply and peacefully together, rooted in this very earth. Her voice, soft yet certain, wove a vision resonating with my hidden longings—a quiet yearning for a different kind of life that I seldom acknowledged.

Her words caused a profound warmth to bloom in my chest, spreading through me like the lingering heat of the wine we had shared, but it was infinitely more potent, resonating with a deeper, almost primal part of me. This astonishing person seemed to reflect my soul's quiet yearning. The fleeting thought of building a life with her, stripped bare of pretence, felt like a distant memory of coming home.

Yet, as I looked at Lee, bathed in the soft, ethereal glow of the moonlight, a different kind of heat stirred within me—a visceral pull that had nothing to do with our shared dreams of a peaceful farm life. It was confusing; I suddenly became sharply aware of her physical presence, which tangled with the deep affection and burgeoning emotional connection I felt. Was it merely the wine casting its intoxicating spell, or was it something more intrinsic, sparked by her vulnerability, closeness, and the unguarded honesty in her eyes? A tremor ran through my hand as I held my glass. Unsure and unsteady, my instinct for self-preservation kicked in, and I decided that retreat was the safest course.

"I should probably call it a night," I murmured, the words feeling clumsy, and inadequate. I hoped my voice wouldn't betray the turmoil churning inside me.

Lee's brow furrowed slightly, a silent question clouding her earnest gaze as I rose. The sudden movement broke the comfortable stillness. "Are you okay, Sunny?" she asked gently, her concern palpable.

She followed me quietly as I moved toward the house, her presence a tangible comfort behind me, the soft rustle of her clothes on the porch the only sound. As I fumbled with the unfamiliar lock of the guest room door and pushed it open, I turned to find her right there, her expression a mix of genuine concern and gentle confusion, her eyes searching mine for an explanation I couldn't articulate. I realized then that my abruptness hadn't gone unnoticed; perhaps it echoed other subtle moments she had found odd in my demeanour.

"You don't have to run," she whispered, her voice low, and intimate, the unspoken hanging heavily between us.

At that moment, almost electric energy filled the thick air. Standing so close, the space between us seemed to hum with a silent vibration. My pulse quickened as a wave of conflicting sensations washed over me—the lingering warmth from Lee's shared dream mingled with a sharp, undeniable attraction that threatened to overwhelm my senses. It felt like standing on the edge of a precipice, where the familiar line between friendship and something far more complex blurred and dissolved before my eyes. Caution battled fiercely with a sudden, primal desire I hadn't anticipated.

A soft sound, barely a whisper of breath, escaped her lips, her gaze unwavering. "Stay?" Her deep brown eyes held mine, not with a command, or a plea, but with an open invitation—a silent promise of shared exploration in their fathomless depths.

Hesitantly, my feet rooted to the spot for a heartbeat longer, I finally stepped back, allowing her entry into the small room.

Without another word, her hand, warm, and surprisingly steady, reached for mine. Her touch sent a pure sensation through me, igniting a fire I didn't know was banked within. Instead of leading me further into the main room, she guided me toward a smaller, more intimate alcove, bathed in soft, diffused light that filtered through the window. The light cast long shadows that danced around us. We stood facing each other, the silence amplifying the frantic beat of my heart and the palpable desire radiating between us like an invisible force. When her fingertips brushed my cheek, light as a moth's wing, a shiver traced down my spine, leaving a trail of goosebumps in its wake. Our eyes locked, and in that shared gaze lay the undeniable potential for a profound and utterly transformative connection—an unspoken understanding passing between us.

Emotion overwhelmed the last remnants of reason. We simultaneously surrendered to an unspoken yearning, our mouths finding each other in a kiss that was both intensely urgent and tentatively exploratory—a first taste of forbidden fruit. I longed for this closeness, this intoxicating connection with Lee, a secret fantasy I had never honestly imagined coming to life. Gently, my hands found the small of her back, guiding her toward the narrow bed. As we sank onto the soft mattress, I deepened the kiss, and the world outside melted away, leaving only the sensation of her lips on mine.

My fingers trembled slightly, as did hers, as I gently eased her soft cotton shirt from her shoulders. It revealed the delicate curve of her collarbone, the smooth slope of her shoulders, and the warm skin beneath. At first, my touch was hesitant. I mapped the contours of her body with newfound reverence, learning her shape as if I were deciphering a language I was only beginning to understand.

Lee responded in kind. Her hands found the buttons of my shirt, her touch gentle yet deliberate as she explored the planes of my chest, igniting sparks of awareness wherever her fingertips grazed. My lips traced slow paths across the sensitive skin of her neck, tasting the faint salt, and warmth. I wanted to commit every inch of her to memory, etching this moment into the deepest recesses of my being.

Her hands, deft and knowing, sought out the places where my breath hitched—sensitive points that sent waves of tingling awareness through my entire body, creating a symphony of sensation.

A low sound, a guttural plea disguised as a command, escaped my throat, raw, and urgent.

"Please... touch me." My voice was rough, barely audible above the frantic pounding of my heart.

"Your hands... I need them."

Her soft palms found me then, closing around my hardness with an exquisite pressure that made me gasp, a sharp intake of breath. Her fingers learned my shape with an intuitive grace, caressing, and exploring with a boldness that thrilled and unnerved me.

"Like this?" she whispered against my heated skin, her breath warm, and intoxicating against my ear.

"Yes," I choked out, arching instinctively into her touch, every nerve ending alive, and singing. "God, Lee..." I buried my face against the curve of her neck, kissing the frantic pulse that beat there, a wild rhythm mirroring my own.

"The way you taste... the way your mouth feels..." I trailed off, words failing to capture the overwhelming intensity of the moment.

She chuckled softly, a low, intimate sound that vibrated against my skin.

"I could explore further, Sunny... uncover all your secrets, if you'd let me."

Her seductive promise ignited a fresh wave of heat coiling low in my belly, a primal response that momentarily overshadowed everything else. The quiet rasp of my belt buckle seemed impossibly loud in the hushed room as her surprisingly steady fingers unfastened it. I stood before her, exposed, and vulnerable, the undeniable evidence of my desire stark in the soft, dim light filtering through the window. Her gaze drifted downward, a slow, appreciative exploration, lingering momentarily on the bead of moisture at my tip. She slowly, reverently, brought her fingertips to her lips, a silent tasting of my anticipation. A slow, knowing smile touched the corners of her mouth, a secret shared between us.

"Mmm," she murmured, her voice husky with desire, sending shivers across my skin, each syllable a caress. "You taste... exquisite."

My control frayed, the carefully constructed walls crumbling. With a groan that rumbled deep in my chest, I helped Lee shrug off the last barrier of her thin lingerie, my mouth finding the soft, yielding swell of her breast. As I worshipped her there, my fingers traced lower, seeking the slick heat I now knew was waiting, finding her wet, and ready. Her sharp intake of breath, a small gasp of pleasure, echoed my ragged sound at the intimate discovery. Bringing my fingers to my lips, her taste – unique, intoxicating, pure Lee – nearly sent me spiralling over the edge of reason.

"You too," I breathed against her heated skin, my voice thick with pure, unadulterated wanting, each word a testament to the intensity of my desire.

"You taste utterly divine, Lee." A fleeting image of Nisha, her familiar scent, flickered at the edge of my awareness, quickly banished by the intoxicating reality of Lee.

My teeth grazed her bottom lip, a playful nip that drew a low, pleased sound from deep in her throat, a sensual rumble that vibrated against my mouth. My hands slid lower, learning the familiar curve of her hips, pulling her flush against me, skin slick against the skin as I guided us together. Pressing into her warmth, entering her felt less like a purely physical act and more like clicking into place, a sense of rightness resonating deep within. A profound understanding of joining, as if two halves of a soul, separated for too long, finally recognized each other's form.

A breathless hiss escaped her lips, her fingers tightening on my shoulders, her nails digging slightly into my skin. "Don't... please, don't stop," she murmured against my ear, the words almost lost in the overwhelming tide of sensation.

Then the rhythm shifted, a subtle arch of her back, a silent invitation. She took the lead, guiding my length against the exquisitely sensitive heart of her pleasure. The friction was electric, a slow burn igniting, and building between us, each movement a spark. She moved with a languid grace at first, then with increasing urgency, drawing out waves of sensation that washed over me, playing my body's responses like a cherished instrument until my control frayed into exquisite, unravelling threads.

A driving need surged through me, a primal urge demanding release. Gently but firmly, I turned Lee to face the cool darkness of the wall, the change in angle intensifying every sensation, every shared breath. My body flushed against her back; I tangled my fingers in the thick silk of her hair, finding a deeper, more primal rhythm within her. Our reflections swam in the shadowed glass of a framed picture nearby—blurred shapes locked in a shared, primal dance, a silent testament to our intertwined bodies. Seeing us like that, lost together in the pulsing cadence, deepened the paradoxical intimacy, the raw need binding us closer even as the world outside ceased to exist.

Later, breathless, and slick with sweat, exhaustion finally claimed us, a heavy weight pulling us down. The intense storm of our passion had ebbed, leaving behind a profound sense of connection—a quiet contentment that settled deep in my bones. Hours might have passed in that timeless space, or perhaps only mere moments; time had lost all meaning, the universe shrinking to the confines of that small bed. I gathered her close, settling her against me, her soft warmth a comforting presence. Even then, it felt like it wasn't enough. I had a desperate longing to hold onto this fragile bubble. I wished we could stay suspended in that moment forever, simply breathing together, my hand stroking the long, tangled strands of her hair while her head rested heavily and trustingly on my chest. Sleep finally took us, our hands loosely clasped, anchoring us in the delicate, stolen peace of the night.

A sharp, unfamiliar noise from outside jolted me awake. Disoriented, I blinked in the pre-dawn gloom, the remnants of shared warmth still clinging to my skin. Lee slept beside me, her face soft, and serene, utterly beautiful in her vulnerability. The tangled sheets and the quiet intimacy of the small room made everything feel intensely real, yet ephemeral, like a dream.

Then reality intruded with painful clarity, a cold wave washing over me. Lee belonged with Jacky, her laughter echoing in another's arms. And I had Nisha's ring heavy on my finger, a constant, silent accusation. A wave of guilt, cold, and sharp, surged through me, extinguishing the lingering embers of our passion. This feeling and connection… was built on a fault line, a dangerous precipice. The guilt of my actions and the overwhelming desire to hold onto this fragile bubble of intimacy battled within me.

I watched her breathe for a moment longer, her chest's gentle rise and fall creating a fragile rhythm. I admired the delicate curve of her cheek and the dark fan of her lashes against her skin. A fleeting memory of Nisha's sleeping face, her familiar stillness, tightened the knot of guilt in my stomach. Gently, I touched Lee's shoulder, a hesitant caress.

"Lee," I whispered, my voice rough from sleep and tinged with a dawning sense of dread. "Wake up. I think I heard something outside."

Her eyes fluttered open, confusion slowly clearing away the remnants of sleep. As awareness returned, I saw it—a flicker of worry, a shadow of understanding, momentarily clouding her soft features. She didn't speak, but the unasked question hung heavy between us, thick with the weight of our actions. What now? What did this mean for everything?

"Hey," I murmured, keeping my voice low, trying to project a calm I didn't truly feel as the adrenaline still coursed beneath my skin.

"Last night... it stays here with us. Okay?"

I met Lee's gaze, silently pleading for understanding, hoping she grasped the unspoken complexities and the absolute necessity of silence. We both understood—this was never supposed to happen, a boundary crossed in the darkness. We were each in committed relationships, anchored in separate harbours. It was a moment of shared temptation that we surrendered to a rogue wave that crashed over our carefully constructed shores. It was a mistake but also a moment of undeniable connection—a spark ignited in the shadows that neither of us could fully explain or ever truly erase. It had to remain buried deep, a secret locked away in the vault of the night.

Checking the clock on the bedside table, I saw the faint green glow that revealed the stark reality: it was five AM. The world outside would soon stir, unaware of the seismic shift that had taken place within these walls. Slipping out of bed as quietly as possible, I moved deliberately, and silently to gather my discarded clothes. Getting dressed felt like putting on armour, piece by piece, with the weight of guilt settling with each button I fastened. I was torn between the desire to stay and the need to leave. Taking one last glance at Lee, who had turned away with her shoulders hunched toward the wall, I slipped out the door, leaving the room, and its intense, complicated memories, along with the lingering scent of her skin, behind me.

A glance into Jackie's room confirmed that he was fast asleep, unclothed, and sprawled amidst a chaotic tangle of sheets. This detail—the sheer abandon of his sleep—sharply lodged in my mind, serving as a disquieting reflection of my thoughts. The coast was clear. I exchanged a silent, almost imperceptible look with Lee, holding our breath in the pre-dawn stillness. She then slipped back into his room like a shadow, rejoining him while I retreated to the relative safety of the hallway.

When I returned to my room, the bed was untouched, the sheets smooth, and undisturbed. A knot of unease tightened in my chest at the emptiness of my space, prompting me to head to the garden, where I found Nisha. She was sitting on a stone bench, facing the awakening landscape. The first rays of dawn painted the sky in soft hues, but her attention seemed elsewhere. She absentmindedly touched her earlobe repetitively, her gaze drifting briefly over the dew-kissed grass near her bare feet as if searching for something small and precious that had been lost. After quickly changing into the comfort of my familiar clothes, I joined her, bracing myself for the inevitable return to normalcy.

Nisha looked up as I approached, her smile dazzling but

perhaps a bit too wide, a brittle brightness around the edges. "Decided to greet the dawn?" she asked lightly, her eyes not quite meeting mine.

I leaned down and kissed her cheek, trying to convey the affection of a practised husband, hoping the familiar gesture would mask the turmoil stirring within me. "Something like that," I murmured, the lie tasting like ash in my mouth. She accepted it, launching into chatter about the beauty of the farm and the crisp morning air, though her earlier distraction lingered subtly beneath her forced enthusiasm, a faint tremor in her voice.

Soon, Jackie, and Lee emerged, the remnants of the previous night clinging to them like a faint perfume. Now dressed in slightly rumpled clothes, Jackie stretched dramatically, a loud, and exaggerated yawn escaping his lips.

"Morning, everyone! I slept like a log," he declared, his voice perhaps a bit too boisterous and cheerful. "Hope I didn't miss anything crucial?" Nisha laughed, the sound too high-pitched, and lacking its usual warmth. "Only our scintillating conversation."

Lee remained quiet, her composure impeccable, her face a carefully constructed mask, but she radiated a subtle, almost palpable tension that only I seemed to notice. We exchanged hollow lies about turning in early, the words hanging like unspoken accusations.

The fragile facade held until Nisha leaned forward, her gaze sharp. "Darling, what happened to your neck?" Her eyes lingered on the telltale mark.

My hand flew to the spot instinctively, the skin still sensitive from the memory of Lee's touch. Lee's passionate bite—the recollection was instantaneous and visceral, a phantom sensation.

"I must have scratched it on a branch," I mumbled, the lie feeling flimsy, and unconvincing even as I said it. My gaze flickered to Lee, who seemed to be studying the intricate flower pattern on her teacup with sudden, intense interest, an act that felt deliberately staged.

"You should be more careful," Jackie said smoothly, his eyes darting between my neck and Lee's averted gaze.

He reached for Lee's hand, where faint red marks stood against her pale wrist. "Looks like the wild got you too, Lee."

Lee pulled her hand away, not snatching it back, but with a deliberate, almost imperceptible firmness, tucking it beneath the soft folds of her shawl. "Just clumsy," she replied, her voice even, and controlled, betraying nothing.

Just then, Jackie reached into his pocket for a handkerchief to wipe the condensation from his water glass. As he pulled it out, something small, and metallic tumbled onto the weathered wooden table with a tiny, significant clink. It was an ornate and unique silver earring, catching the morning light. Jackie frowned at it, a brief flicker of confusion crossing his face as if he didn't recognize it, before casually pocketing it again. My eyes instantly turned to Nisha. She wore only one earring—the intricate silver design perfectly matched the fallen back. The earlier image of her searching in the grass and touching her earlobe solidified the damning connection between them. Lee and I needed no words; we silently acknowledged our mirrored betrayals, a mutual understanding that sent a chill down my spine.

The air crackled with unspoken accusations like a silent storm gathering overhead. Perhaps sensing the shift in mood—or flustered by the near discovery of her missing earring—Nisha abruptly changed the subject, her movements just a touch too brisk.

"Oh, you know what I found this morning, right on the little table just outside Jackie's patio door?" she said, reaching into her bag with a smile that was just a little too bright. She pulled out Stars In You and Me and held it up like a prize.

Her gaze locked on Lee, the gesture oddly theatrical—too deliberate.

"Isn't this the poetry book you love, Lee? Such a coincidence! I was thinking of borrowing it."

Lee froze. Her breath caught, her knuckles whitening around her teacup, and her other hand curled into a fist beneath her shawl.

"That's... my copy," she said, voice calm but tight, each word carved out of stone. "I left it… near our bedside table."

Flustered by Lee's uncharacteristic tone—and perhaps sensing the unspoken current beneath her words—Jackie jumped in with a rushed, clumsy attempt at deflection.

"Oh! Right! I must have picked it up to glance through it last night, Lee. Forgot I left it out there. Nisha must've just spotted it this morning. My mistake!"

However, his explanation clashed with Nisha's earlier claim of having randomly found the book, the contradiction hanging awkwardly in the air.

The tension thickened, and small cracks began to web across the surface of their delicate facade, exposing something brittle beneath.

Lee's book. Found outside Jackie's door that morning.

Nisha's missing earring tumbled from Jackie's pocket.

The pieces didn't simply fall into place; they *slammed* together with the weight of a physical blow, shattering the fragile illusion of normalcy. The noise from Jackie's room, the unsettling image of him naked, the half-truths we told about the previous night, the marks on our skin—silent testimonies. It wasn't a parallel play or separate Sins in the Dark. It was a *mirrored betrayal—*

perfect in its symmetry, devastating in its truth.

The four of us sat frozen in the soft glare of morning light, the silence between us heavy and suffocating. One easy and practised, the smiles had vanished, replaced by masks of strained neutrality, slipping at the edges.

Every glance was a confession. Every breath is an indictment.

The illusion of a carefree weekend lay in ruins around us. And in its place: a poisoned silence, thick with the weight of our shared shame.

Author's Note

Dear Readers,

I am thrilled to have you join me on this incredible journey through my trilogy. Your presence here means the world to me, and I hope you find joy, intrigue, and connection as you explore the pages of my books.

"Sizzling With Next" delves into the intimate lives of housewives, presenting ten captivating narratives. These stories unravel the challenges they face in their quest for romantic fulfilment and explore the unspoken desires hidden within their relationships. It's a thought-provoking journey that will leave you reflecting on the complexities of love and passion.

"Sizzling With She 2 She" shifts the lens to the delicate intricacies of the lesbian community. Through ten poignant tales, this volume beautifully captures the profound emotions, struggles, and triumphs of love, and connection in its many forms.

Within these pages, you encountered stories that captured the many shades of love. I trust they stirred something within you and left behind thoughts that gently linger.

Life often presents us with challenges, but amidst the trials, the desire for love, and connection remains a universal truth. This trilogy explores various themes and perspectives, all emphasizing the importance of human connection and the transformative power of understanding.

Communication is the cornerstone of any strong relationship. As we navigate life's twists and turns, having someone to talk to—someone who listens and understands—is invaluable. Open and honest dialogue is vital in any marriage or partnership, as is supporting each other through life's highs and lows. Together, we can overcome obstacles, and strengthen our bonds.

I would love to hear your thoughts and reflections on this journey. Your feedback is invaluable to me. If you'd like to share, please tag me on Instagram **@kazishaheen**—I look forward to connecting with you there!

May these stories inspire hope, understanding, and deeper connections, illuminating the path to lasting love and meaningful relationships.

With warm regards and heartfelt gratitude,

Shaheen Kazi